Clarice Bean,
Don't Look Now

Lauren Child

CANDLEWICK PRESS
CAMBRIDGE, MASSACHUSETTS

PART ONE

Thinking and Spinning

Where does infinity end?

For a long time I used to go to bed early.

But now I go to bed late.

I am not sleeping at night.

And I wake up in the dark.

And my mind is thinking and spinning.

And I start to go into a panic.

And that's when I have to switch on my Ruby flashlight—I keep it by my bed.

It's in the shape of a piece of wood.

It's disguised, like most Ruby things.

I am currently reading **THE RUBY REDFORT SURVIVAL HANDBOOK: WHAT TO DO WHEN YOUR WORST WORRY COMES YOUR WAY.**

Granny sent it to me—you can't buy it over here in this country, not yet.

It is a very handy book and it is crammed with brilliant ideas.

Most of them seem to involve standing still.

For instance, what to do if a tiger comes along—stand still.

And the whole book is about escaping or getting out of and dealing with tricky situations.

You wouldn't believe some of the tricky situations Ruby can get into, and although it is unlikely that I will find myself in a swamp with an alligator, who can say that I won't?

And what I always think is, I would rather know something than not know something.

Don't you think?

I have quite a few worries. I have made a list of them in my notebook—it's a notebook for **worst worries**—because people say things aren't so bad if you make a list.

And then you can check things off when they are solved. So far I haven't checked anything off.

When I first started my Worst Worry Notebook, WORRY no. 1 *was* how to stop my brother Minal from eating all the chocolate cookies before I got home from school.

But then Mom stopped buying chocolate cookies because she said all our teeth would fall out. So the worry sort of went away—though it doesn't count as solved.

Lately I have been having bigger worries—for example, i.e., WORRY no. 4: the meaning of life.

Why are we here?

Is it just to be nice to everybody and have a nice time? Or do we all have to come up with something clever—like doing a test or something.

On one program I heard, they said space goes on and on forever without stopping.

And how it has no edges.

And they call it infinity.

But what I want to know is, how can something go on and on forever without stopping?

How can something have no edges?

Am I just a tiny speck floating about with lots of other specks,

i.e., planets and stars?

Where does infinity end?

WORRY no. 1: infinity.

Mom says, "It is often best not to think too much about it because it is all slightly beyond our understanding and if you spend too long wondering about it all, it can make you feel rather insignificant," i.e., small and pointless.

Which to be honest I do feel a lot of the time anyway. I phone Granny and ask her, does she ever feel small and pointless when she thinks about infinity?

And she says, "Not a bit of it; I love infinity. It's rather reassuring to remember you are just a speck and that in the end it really doesn't matter if you wear a pair of purple shoes with a red coat or a pair of yellow ones."

I ask Grandad—he says, "The last time I was there I lost my glasses but on the whole I'm for it."

Dad says, "I am sure it would be a quieter place to read the paper."

Which I am not sure is true because I believe there is a lot of wind in space.

One thing I do know is,
the more you worry, the more worries there are,
and just when you get used to things, they change.

WORRY no. 3: change.

Things have a habit of not being the same quite a lot.

Change can be a good thing for some people, but sometimes it comes along when you don't want it to.

Like when my teacher Mrs. Nesbit changed into Mrs. Wilberton.

Or when my mom and dad decided to stop having three children and have four instead, and we got Minal.

And I stopped being the youngest and became the second from youngest—and being the second from youngest isn't really anything, is it?

Just three out of four.

Mom says I will see the benefit of him when I get a bit older.

I say, "When did you see the benefit of Uncle Ted?"

And she says, "When I left home."

But the thing I am trying to say is, change can mess up how you fit into things.

And you never know when change is going to happen.

Which means you never know when disaster is going to strike.

There is this bit in **THE RUBY REDFORT SURVIVAL HANDBOOK** which is worrying me. Right at the end of the first chapter Ruby says, "REMEMBER—it's the worry you haven't even thought to worry about—that is the worry that should worry you the most."

I am wondering what Ruby means—should I be worrying about everything just in case it might be my worst worry? And I am thinking if this is true then I am going to have to get a bigger notebook.

And I think, how can you stop your worst worry from coming your way if you don't know what your worst worry could be?

What to do when Disaster Strikes

You see, the whole problem starts because Marcie is running a bath while she is also talking on the phone and she forgets that she has the faucet turned on and is just nonstop chatting with her friend Stan—Stan is a girl even though it doesn't sound like it and she mainly wears boys' clothes.

Anyway she is chatting so much that she forgets the bath, and the next thing you know, I am watching the television and finding it's raining into my Snackle Pops.

Of course it takes me a few minutes to work out what is going on until I hear Minal shouting, "The carpet in our bedroom is all soggy." I go in there and he is jumping up and down on it in his bare feet like an utter lunatic.

When Marcie realizes, she screams because she knows she will be in for it and in very big trouble.

Grandad is asleep in his chair and does not realize he has gone a bit damp at the edges until he wakes up.

He says, "It is funny, but I was dreaming I was in India during the monsoon."

What Ruby would say is, **"When disaster strikes, stay calm and work as a team. Someone must take charge."**

Marcie starts shouting at Minal. She says, "Why didn't you turn the faucet off, creep!" I say, "It's not his fault, you're the one who wasn't paying attention."

Of course Minal is quite surprised that I am defending him—as I normally do not. Marcie says, "A lot of good you are, just sitting watching TV all the time."

I say, "At least I don't cause Grandad to get all saturated in water—he might get a chill."

Kurt says, "Marcie, why are you blaming everyone else when it is your stupid fault?"

Marcie says, "Why don't you go and call one of your drip girlfriends?"

And he says, "I would if I could ever manage to get the phone off you—is it Super-Glued to your ear?"

And then Marcie says something very rude and they get in an argument.

When Dad gets home, he makes a wincing face while he is listening to Marcie talking very, very fast about the happenings that have led up to this disaster.

Dad finally puts her out of her misery by saying, "OK, I gather from all this babbling that the soggy state of our home is due to you, but these things happen and who cannot put up their hand and say, 'I have overflowed a bath'?"

I want to put up my hand and say, *"I have never overflowed a bath"* but I am confused as to whether putting up my hand means I have or means I haven't—so I keep quiet.

Dad says, "Marce, if you just say you are sorry, that can be the end of it."

Marcie says, "I am sorry."

Dad says, "Fine, fetch a mop."

We all find ourselves doing a lot of mopping— even Grandad.

He says it reminds him of his Navy days when he used to have to scrub the decks.

Dad says, "You were never *in* the Navy."

Grandad says, "No, you are quite right; I must have been thinking of that movie I watched last week."

Anyway, by the time Mom gets home, everything is shipshape and there is no mess at all.

But it doesn't take her long to realize something has happened—Mom is a bit like this.

She has a sixth sense for trouble.

She says, "So who's going to tell me what small disaster occurred while I was out?"

Nobody says anything, but strangely there is a cracking noise and some powdery dust sprinkles down from above us.

Then there is a crashing sound and before we know what the dickens is going on, the ceiling is on the carpet.

Luckily it is not the ceiling above us or we would all be knocked out and possibly squashed and dead.

Mom squints at Dad, and Dad winces at Marcie, and Marcie bites her lip.

Of course, the person to call is Uncle Ted.

Uncle Ted comes over on the double because he is used to being phoned one minute and arriving the next.

You see, Uncle Ted is a fireman and he is good in an emergency.

Dad and Kurt and Uncle Ted clear up all the rubble.

Unfortunately what we discover is that the television is a goner.

It was all quite exciting and out of the ordinary until that happened, but now it is an utter disaster and a tragedy.

It's like Ruby Redfort says: "Sometimes you will find you have a piece of equipment so vital that you will be totally lost without it—in other words, it is essential to your survival."

If you do find yourself with your most vitalist piece of equipment destroyed, then Ruby Redfort would say, "You must either improvise or seek out an alternative."

So of course I take her advice and call my best friend, Betty Moody, immediately.

And she says, "Come over any time."

So I say, "I'll be there first thing tomorrow."

Every Spy needs an Accomplice

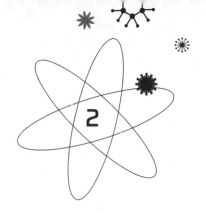

The next morning I find Marcie sitting on the kitchen table with her friend Stan. They are painting each other's fingernails blue—it doesn't look that nice.

I say, "Where is everybody?"

Marcie says, "Mom's at work, Dad isn't home, Kurt's at the shop, Grandad's asleep, and Minal's playing with your Ruby flashlight."

I say, "*What?* Why didn't you stop him?"

Marcie shrugs, she says, "I didn't think you would mind."

Which is a big fat lie because she certainly *does* know I would mind.

I race up the stairs and find him trying to glue it back together using that glue tiny children use for sticking paper—it can't even stick a tissue, so I don't know why he thinks it will be able to stick a actual flashlight.

When he sees me, he looks utterly sheepish.

He even says, "Sorry," but I am not in the mood for sorry—I just give him my worst look and go off to Betty Moody's.

Luckily she recently arrived back from San Francisco where she has been having a vacation with her mom and dad, call-me-Cecil and call-me-Mol. What's strange is they left Mol behind. When I asked Betty why, she just said, "No reason."

Which is odd because why would you
leave someone of your family
behind for no reason?

Betty has a TV in her own actual bedroom—so we just lie on beanbags mostly watching the Ruby Redfort show and chatting about things that happen at school and what we would do if we didn't have to go to school.

Almost as soon as I arrive, Betty says, "Hey, how did you get that?"

She is talking about my Ruby Redfort secret fly badge—they are really hard to get hold of—you send off for them and only a few people are chosen to have one.

You have to sew it onto your scarf or hat or pocket or somewhere—not too obvious because as Ruby says, "A true spy will notice the unnoticeable."

Mine is inside my coat and hardly possible to see but I am not surprised that Betty noticed it—Betty Moody is mainly always noticing the unnoticeable.

I am pleased Betty is back because I need her help with the detective secret agent series I have been writing over summer vacation. The main character is called Macey Gruber. She has an accomplice named Florence Antwater, and her catch phrase is Don't look now—as in, "Don't look now, but I think we got company,"—or "Don't look now, but some bozo just stole your car."

The problem is coming up with a twist—you always need a twist if you are writing a detective secret agent story—but it is not always possible to think of one. Betty says we should talk to our drama workshop teacher, Czarina, about it—Betty says Czarina would probably tell us to do some improvising because this might help us have inspiration.

While we are planning what to improvise, we read some of Betty's Ruby books.

She has all of them—and we have read them all at least three times. There is a new series called the Ruby Redfort handbooks. Betty has got this latest one in California, called

THE RUBY REDFORT SPY GUIDE: HOW TO KNOW THINGS WITHOUT KNOWING THINGS.

It explains how there is all this information which people are always giving out whether they like it or not and from it you can work out all kinds of things that they wouldn't dream of telling you themselves. Like often, when people are lying to you, they look up at the sky.

So Ruby says the golden rule thing to remember is, "You gotta read between the lines."

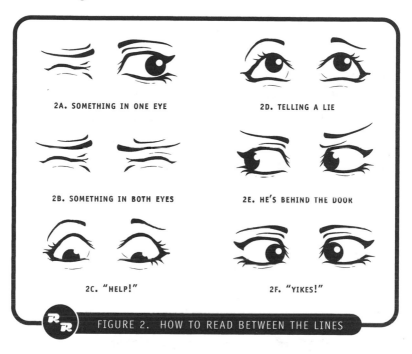

2A. SOMETHING IN ONE EYE

2D. TELLING A LIE

2B. SOMETHING IN BOTH EYES

2E. HE'S BEHIND THE DOOR

2C. "HELP!"

2F. "YIKES!"

FIGURE 2. HOW TO READ BETWEEN THE LINES

Betty says, "She's *right*. For example, like when people are blinking a lot, does it mean they are signaling to someone? Or that they are nervous? Or that maybe they have a nervous twitch?"

I say, "Or even they could have something in their *actual eye*."

Betty says, "*Exactly*."

One thing that really always annoys me is when someone says,

"Clarice Bean, you are going all red—are you all embarrassed?"

OR "Clarice Bean, you are going all red— what mischief have you been getting into?"

And it doesn't always mean you are embarrassed or up to mischief. Sometimes it means you have accidentally swallowed a cough drop and can't breathe.

And sometimes it means you are thinking, *Oh no there's that person who always says, "Why are you going all red?"*—and this can make you furious, which makes you go all red.

I say, "Betty, I am finding this book really fascinating and exceptionordinarily interesting and probably quite useful."

Betty says, "Would you like to borrow it? I don't need it right now."

I say, "Are you sure?"

And Betty says, "*Sure* I'm sure."

And I say, "Thanks a whole lot, that would be great."

Betty is a really generous person and she may have a lot of nice things that I really want but she will always share them.

After we have watched five Ruby episodes including our favorite one called

You Better Believe It, Baby,

I decide to head off home.

We are standing on the doorstep and I am about to say good-bye, when Betty nudges me and says, "Don't look now, but there goes Robert Granger."

He lives next door and he is always trying to talk to me and he is always telling people what I have been up to. I am relieved she warned me, because if he had seen me, I would have to walk home with him. It reminds me of something Ruby always says: "Every Spy needs an Accomplice."

On my way home I realize that the TV being squashed is not such a worst worry after all because I can always go and watch it at Betty's.

Never eat a Polar Bear's liver — no matter how hungry you are

On my way back home, I flick through the pages of the **SPY GUIDE** and read this chapter called THE HUMAN FACE NEVER STOPS TALKING.

Ruby says, "Your eyes are the key to unlocking someone else's brain. Your archenemy may not be saying a word, but you can bet your bottom dollar his face will tell you everything you wanna know."

When I get home, I use this technique on Minal Cricket.

It works like a charm because when I say, "Where have you hidden the mini doughnuts, you creep," he says, "Not telling," but when he says it, he looks over at the washing machine and right away I know where they are.

They are in my grasp in a millisecond.

He says, "How did you know that?"

And I say, "Because] can read you like a book, baby." It's the kind of thing that Ruby would say to the arch villain Hogtrotter.

When I go upstairs later, I notice that all my bedding has been jumbled up and there is an actual live worm on my pillow.

To get my revenge, I put Minal's pajamas in the toilet and flush it.

This causes another flood, which makes Mom *utterly* livid.

Then Dad calls and says he will not be coming home from work for the foreseeable next few hours due to his boss Mr. Thorncliff making him work too hard.

Mom says she is at her wits' end and has had enough of this house and she's not feeling too crazy about some of the people who live in it either.

Marcie goes and runs her a bath because this usually does the trick with calming Mom down but unfortunately the bathroom door falls off—probably due to people banging their fists on it all the time— and so this just makes things worse.

She says, "I am going to see my friend Suki. I may be some time."

And just like that, we have to get our own supper, which is mainly cheese.

When Mom gets home, she makes an announcement. I am expecting her to say, "Due to bad behavior and too many arguments, mini doughnuts will be banned."

But she doesn't.

She says, "Due to the stove being wrecked by the ceiling falling on it and me being up to my ears in work down at the old persons' center—mainly due to our new resident, Mr. Larsson, demanding herring every five minutes—I am afraid you are all going to have to start making your own supper.
I suggest toast."

Marcie gives me and Minal a look and says, "This is your fault, brats."

Which I think is typically not true and unfair.

When I go to bed—a little bit hungry—I realize that perhaps THE WORST WORRY I DIDN'T EVEN THINK TO WORRY ABOUT is having to eat toast for the rest of my life.

I write this worry down in my Worst Worry Notebook.

WORRY no. 11: Can one
live off toast
alone?

The next day things aren't much better.

Not only is it very difficult to get any privacy in the bathroom but also my mother is not in a much gooder mood.

Mom says to Dad,

"I am fed up with you working late all the time."

Dad says, "So am I."

Mom says, "I am fed up with this rotten house."

Dad says, "So am I."

Mom says, "I am fed up with everybody arguing all the time."

Dad says, "So am I."

Mom says, "I am fed up with you saying 'So am I.'"

Dad says, "So am I, but I can't help agreeing with you."

Mom says, "Well, if you agree with me so much, will you please do something?"

Dad gives her a squeeze and says,
"You bet I will, kid."

Which is exactly the kind of thing Ruby Redfort's butler, Hitch, would say if he was here now.

Which I wish he was because he is good at fixing things and would certainly not allow people to eat toast all the time.

It is getting toward lunchtime and I end up having to eat a piece of celery and a small spreadable cheese.

I decide that I must find an alternative food supply—so I take a page out of Ruby's book and I use my resources.

WHAT TO DO WHEN FOOD IS SCARCE.

Ruby says, "When food is scarce, take advantage of any opportunities that come your way—if you are hungry, you will not be able to think fast, and in a survival situation, thinking fast might just save your bacon.

N.B. Never eat a polar bear's liver—no matter how hungry you are."

Not that you will most likely get the chance because he will be too busy eating yours.

I phone up Betty Moody and ask her if I can go over there for lunch.

Betty says, "Yes, of course, we will be going to Manic Organic—it's a fast food organic café."
I call out to Mom, who is somewhere in the actual house but who knows where and ask her if it will be fine for me to go out for lunch rather than stay in eating toast.

And she says, "If I could, I would, so why not?"

A Secret is only a Secret when it is Secret

On my way out of the house, I spot this red envelope—it is slightly tucked under the doormat, which is why I almost didn't see it. I pick it up and I catch sight of something reflecting in the light.

And when I look closely, I see the shiny thing is a fly printed on in varnish—it is almost invisible. This means only one thing—it is something to do with Ruby Redfort. Inside are four tickets to the movie of Ruby Redfort, called

Run, Ruby, Run.

I am allowed me, 2 adults, and one child. They aren't tickets for going to the movie like a normal person.

They are for the premiere and it is at Christmas.

If you don't know it, why I have got this

invitation is because I was slightly talent-spotted and in fact in the *actual* Ruby Redfort movie, playing quite a smallish part. No speaking—just reacting.

I learned how to do reacting from my drama teacher, Czarina. It's much more difficult than you would think—the secret is to not overdo it. Anyway it is very exciting that I will be watching myself in an actual real-life movie and I will get to meet Skyler Summer again—the actual Ruby Redfort actress.

Of course I don't even have to think about who I will take, because it will utterly definitely be Betty Moody.

THE PREMIERE OF

Run, Ruby, Run

A *RUBY REDFORT* PRODUCTION

ADMIT ONE

LOCATION, TIME, & DRESS CODE CONTAINED SOMEWHERE ON THIS DOCUMENT

Be there, buster.

It is the first time I have ever had a really exciting thing to take Betty Moody to—normally it is her who invites me to good things, so I decide I will keep it a secret so I can surprise her on the day.

What I know about secrets is that it is very hard to keep them a secret. Ruby has good advice about this problem in her **SPY GUIDE**—the main thing to do is to tell as few people as necessary. She says,

"REMEMBER, people love telling secrets.
So RULE ONE: Keep your trap shut.
RULE TWO: Never tell a blabbermouth."

I know all about this rule because I have my younger brother, Minal Cricket, who is a little big-mouth and always telling things when he is not supposed to. Anyway, just before I go off to meet Betty, I race around the place trying to find Mom—she is sitting in a closet trying to sort out shoes and decide which ones she could throw out—it turns out to be five pairs of Dad's and one pair of hers. When I tell her about the tickets, she is very excited and decides that the shoes she is throwing out might be good for a premiere and she should keep them after all.

I phone Dad at work but he is in a meeting so I

leave a message with Miss Egglington, his assistant—she says, "*Sounds important. I will get a message to him immediately.*"

On my walk to Manic Organic, I am thinking about how it will be really hard to not say anything because I normally tell Betty Moody nearly everything.

Me and Betty and call-me-Cecil have a very nice lunch at Manic Organic, although it is actually not very manic or fast and although the people behind the counter are doing lots of shouting out things like,

"One couscous,
two alfalfa, and
a celery juice" we do wait
47 minutes before we get all the things we ordered. And I am feeling a bit delirious with hunger. I ask call-me-Cecil where call-me-Mol has gone, but he doesn't seem to want to talk about it and Betty gets all fidgety—which is a bit odd and then I think it is a bit odd that Mol has stayed behind in San Francisco without him—they always travel in a pair. And then I think maybe they don't want to talk about it because Cecil and Mol are getting a divorce.

Cecil doesn't seem like someone getting a divorce

but then I don't know how people are meant to seem when they are getting a divorce, so I wouldn't know. And this must be Betty Moody's WORST WORRY, THE WORRY SHE DIDN'T EVEN THINK TO WORRY ABOUT.

Afterward we hang out at Betty's until it is time to go to drama workshop. We are walking down the road when I suddenly say, "Don't look now, but there's Justin Broach."

Justin Broach is this boy at our school—he's not in my year—he's older. He is quite tall, tall for his age—and he thinks he is so good-looking and Grace Grapello agrees with him. Most people do. It is best to agree with Justin Broach—he will most likely give you a Chinese burn if you don't. He never gets in trouble for anything because he is the kind of boy that grown-ups always think is really nice even though he most likely spends his time pulling the wings off flies. He always walks along with this other boy who has an odd haircut. He is always looking at Justin Broach—it's a sort of waiting kind of look—a bit like how a dog looks at its owner when he is hoping for a stick to be thrown.

Betty Moody and me try to keep out of their way because Ruby Redfort always says, "IF TROUBLE IS AROUND THE CORNER, TRY WALKING THE OTHER WAY."

And so even though they are just specks in the distance, we watch out for which direction they are going in.

Czarina is looking a bit tired after her summer vacation and is not doing her usual nipping about in bare feet.

We try out some of our improvisations on her and she says, "Darlinks—you are being too logical about this, too literal; you are stifling your creative urges; you are suffocating your free spirits. Drama is not something to be boxed up like a caged animal."

She says, "Be a bit more *avant-garde**"— which I would try to be if I knew what it meant— all I know is that it is foreign. But I will look it up in my dictionary when I get home.

Czarina does her own improvisation to show us what she means and I suddenly understand what she is trying to tell us and I think she really is exceptionordinarily good when it comes to drama.

* Avant-garde: *doing something in an exceptionordinarily modern and different way.*

I am dying to tell her about the Ruby Redfort premiere and how she can go and see me in the actual cinema and if I had another ticket for an adult, I would take her. But Betty Moody might hear because Czarina would utterly definitely say,

"Darlink! You are too fabulous"

in a very loudish voice.

When I get home after drama workshop, Dad is sitting there in his smartest suit. He says, "So I hear you're in the movies, kid."

People often say they are kidding when in fact they aren't kidding at all

5

The next morning I go into the kitchen and scout about for something more nourishing like maybe an egg. And I think of the Ruby **SURVIVAL HANDBOOK** where she explains how to find a morsel to eat when you are in the middle of a barrenish desert. It turns out it is possible, but you have to know where to look—there are plants that are full of vital goodness and others that will kill you of poison in seconds. I look in the fridge and there is a tomato that is no longer a tomato and more like a white furry blob and I am sure is now actually in fact possibly a killer.

Dad is on the phone going, "Really—you are booked up till when? . . . *Really*? . . . So there is no way you could start before January? . . . *Really?*

Well, how about just coming over and giving us a quote? . . . You can't come till when? . . . *November?*"

Mom's face is tipped to one side and she looks slightly in pain.

Dad puts the phone down and gives her a look that according to the **SPY GUIDE** means, **"I tried, I really did—you heard me trying, didn't you?"**

Mom says, "I just don't think I can put up with this for another three months."

And Dad says, "Why don't we just abandon the house and go and live in a Travelodge?"

Mom says, "If you are joking, watch out, because I am tempted."

Dad says, "Oh, I'm not joking—which Travelodge do you fancy?"

Mom says, "Any one with a bathroom door." This is the kind of conversation that gives me the shivers. Because you see they are joking about us moving and leaving this house. I don't like people joking about this sort of thing.

Moving is not funny; it is—

WORRY no. 3: change.

And what Ruby Redfort says is,
"People often say they are kidding when in fact they are not really kidding."

She also says, "When people are getting on your nerves, it is a good idea to get some air."

I decide this is very good advice and put on my coat and walk up toward the hill. On the way, I bump into Betty Moody. She is hurrying along with her dog, Ralph—he is a Pekingese. She whispers, "Don't look now, but Justin Broach is coming this way." We quickly dodge into Eggplant, the organic vegetarian shop where Kurt works, usually with this girl called Kira.

I like it there. It's sort of calming and you can drink herbal drinks at the counter.

In the shop it's all quiet—i.e., no customers.

Kurt and Kira are sitting on the counter throwing kidney beans into an old tin.

There are beans all over the floor because the beans mostly bounce out.

Kira keeps saying, "You totally suck, Kurt"— Kira's from New York.

And then Kurt grabs Kira and sort of pins her arm

behind her back and she says, "I take it back, *I take it back.*"

It's very difficult to talk to them because they are too interested in each other to be interested in anyone else. Even Betty seems to have gone into a sort of   T R A N C E   and is just staring at them. I am relieved when Waldo Park, who is the owner, comes back into the shop because at least you can get to talk to a normalish person who isn't all besotted with another besotted person.

Waldo Park looks at the beans and then he looks at Kurt and Kira and he says, "It looks like you two have been kidneying around."

Waldo Park asks us if we would like to arrange the shelves—he says we can do it however we like. So we do it by the colors of the containers.

The bottles of vitamins look really nice next to the tinned artichokes and they look super good next to butter beans. And the butter beans look really pleasing next to the environmentally friendly washing powder. And the washing powder looks right when it is next to the blue corn chips.

Waldo Park says it is an inspired arrangement of

merchandise and it might make people think twice when they are buying their groceries.

And also it might encourage people to eat chips while they are doing their laundry.

He says he will let us know if sales are up next week. When we have finished, Waldo Park gives us a tofu burger and we sit on the shop assistants' stools. I notice Karl Wrenbury walk by, and he is with his brother Alf who wears glasses. They have five dogs.

It's because their mom has this dog-walking business and Karl sometimes helps her out.

I stick my head out of the door and say, "Hey, Karl, if you are going to the hill with all those dogs, we'll come."

He says, "OK, get me a cookie."

I put my coat on and scrabble about to find my gloves, which have dropped on the floor—Ralph is chewing them.

When I look up, I am surprised that Betty is still sitting on her stool.

I say, "Aren't you coming?"

And she says, "No, Ralph is tired—I think we'll go home."

I say, "He doesn't look tired." Because he doesn't—he never does.

And she says, "Well, I am not really in the mood."

What does she mean, "not in the mood"? Betty Moody isn't a moody type of a person. I wonder what is wrong. And then I remember about Betty Moody's WORST WORRY—THE WORRY SHE DIDN'T EVEN THINK TO WORRY ABOUT.

And that she is probably not in the mood because of Cecil and Mol getting a divorce.

It makes me want to tell her about the **Run, Ruby, Run** tickets—it would cheer her up at least a bit even if Cecil and Mol are divorcing from each other.

But I keep zipped and instead just say, "I'll see you on Monday." And she just nods.

It is a lovely day and the sun is shining through the leaves and even though it is beginning to be autumn it isn't that cold.

I have a nice time with Karl and Alf and although Alf is much younger than me, he is nothing like my younger brother and he is really funny and he also knows about things.

And when I say how you should never eat a polar bear's liver if you can possibly help it, he says, "That's because they are poisonous to actual humans."

He says, "Also you should never eat just only rabbits because it takes more vitamins to digest a rabbit than it gives you vitamins to eat one."

Alf says, "Not that I would eat a rabbit anyway because I really like them and I have one in our garden—called Nibbles."

When I get home, Marcie is flipping through one of those magazines about other people's homes.

Mom looks over her shoulder and says, "Oh, nice house, huh?"

And Marcie says, "*Mmm,* I wish we had a bathroom with underfloor heating." And Mom says, "I wish we had a bathroom with a floor."

And Marcie says, "I wish I had a bathroom all to myself."

And Mom says, "Right now I wouldn't mind a house all to myself, any house, so long as it's not this house."

I am quite shocked that she would say this about our house.

I look around and notice nothing has changed—
the bathroom door is still missing, the ceiling still has
a big hole, and due to no stove it's still cheese-on-
toast for snack.

I can't help thinking that if you offered me a
rabbit for dinner, *I might just eat it.*

I go to bed and manage to get to sleep in fact
quite quickly but I am woken up in the middle of
the night by a strange edgy feeling and by the
morning it is still there.

It is like that oddish sensation you sometimes get
when you know something bad is lurking about at
the back of your mind but you can't put your finger
on what it is.

Even after I have checked my face for felt-
tipping—because Minal sometimes draws a mustache
on me while I am asleep—the feeling keeps nagging
away.

And I am wondering if it is THE WORST WORRY
I DIDN'T EVEN THINK TO WORRY ABOUT.

How to deal with your Most Trickiest Person

The next day is the last day of the summer vacation—
it has all rushed by very quickly. And today I have to
go with Mom to the old persons' center to help her
make some posters and things. You see, she and my
headmaster, who is called Mr. Pickering, have come
up with this idea for the people at my school to visit
the old persons' center and make them a cup of tea.

It's a Christmas type of a thing about being
friendly to people you don't actually know. They're
drawing names from a hat so you don't know who
you are going to get. It's voluntary—i.e., you don't
have to do it—except I do because I am Mom's
daughter and it would look a bit mean if I didn't. In
any case I would do it anyway because I like visiting
and it will be in pairs so I can go with Betty. You

can meet lots of interesting people you wouldn't normally see out and about in the everyday world.

I run into the shop opposite Eggplant, called Foxes—Mom loiters about outside because she doesn't want Waldo Park to see her go in there—he is against Foxes because it is a rival shop and it is open till 10 at night and he is worried everyone will buy their milk in there and stop bothering to buy it in his shop and they won't care whether it is organic or not. Because in the end people would rather have convenience than be organic.

Unfortunately we don't have any choice; we have to go into Foxes because we need some raspberry shortcakes for Mr. Flanders and you can't buy them in Eggplant as Waldo Park doesn't stock them due to him thinking they are too sugary. When I come out, Mom is peering in the real estate agent's window. She is really concentrating and I have to tap her on the arm to make her notice me. And I notice that the strange edgy feeling from the middle of the night has crept back.

When we get to the center, we get to work right away. Once I have designed my posters, I go and find Mr. Enkledorf. He is one of my favorite people to visit because he has several parakeets. We usually talk about them and his dead dog called Dudley.

After four cups of tea—which I only drink to be polite—I am really needing a trip to the toilet, but I am just about to skip off down the hall when I hear Mr. Larsson's door open at the end of the corridor. I almost walked straight into him—
this is why you need an accomplice or Betty to say, "Don't look now, but look who it is."

I have heard all about him from Mom. She has warned me to keep out of Mr. Larsson's way as he is very difficult and can be quite tricky. Ruby has a good bit in her **SURVIVAL HANDBOOK** about dealing with unfriendly types.

She says, "When dealing with unfriendly persons, it is usually wisest to kill 'em with kindness—this makes it very difficult for them to get into a fight with you."

She says the rule is, "Grin until it hurts."

Unfortunately, I have not mastered this Ruby technique, so I wait until I think he has walked down the corridor—this takes quite a long time because Mr. Larsson has a walker—I can hear it clattering.

By the time he has creaked off, it is almost too late and I am lucky to make it to the toilet in time.

We get home quite late-ish and I am brushing my teeth in the kitchen because someone is in the bathroom and I am thinking to myself that perhaps I will start to enjoy school again—like I did with Mr. Washington. Mr. Washington was the exchange teacher we had last summer—and he said that maybe I could be a good writer some day. Maybe even do it for a job. So I think perhaps people would be very interested in my worst worries book and when I have finished it I might get it in the shops like Ruby Redfort's one. And you see, maybe I will like having our new teacher almost as much as I liked having Mr. Washington and perhaps I might stop having so many worries because

WORRY no. 5:
Mrs. Wilberton
will be knocked off the list.

I am walking upstairs daydreaming about my new life at school and how the new teacher might be the only one to discover that in fact I am a math genius after all.

I notice that for once I don't have the usual dreading feeling about going back to school. And I look at my **Worst Worries Notebook** and wonder if I should cross out **WORRY no. 7: having to go back to school after summer vacation** because finally we will not be having Mrs. Wilberton honking at us ever again and there will be a new teacher who cannot possibly be nearly as bad even if it turned out to be Mom's most trickiest person, Mr. Larsson, or even Ruby Redfort's archenemy, Count Von Viscount.

Even then I would be able to say,

"What an improvement."

There is no greater Surprise than the Surprise of the Familiar

7

It is quite nice to be back at school and see some of the people I like—my cousin Noah, Suzie Woo, Lucy Mackay, people like that but mainly Karl and Betty—who although I have seen them quite a bit in the summer, it somehow feels like I haven't seen them for ages when I see them now.

I do have to go the long way around to get to my peg, though, because Justin Broach is lurking in the corridor and I don't feel like getting a Chinese burn on my first day back at school.

Mainly being back is all very pleasant for a change—for one thing we have a different classroom, which turns out to be much nicer than the old one because it gets more sun and I need more sun.

I am sitting next to Betty as usual and we are

chatting about how she has heard that we are going
to be getting Miss Meyer—although she will be
called Mrs. Kelp as she has gotten married over the
summer. What I do know is she is not a shouter and
I have heard also quite a good teacher too so I am
not at all worried.

Until Betty Moody whispers, "Don't look now,
but look who it is," and I look up and am surprised
by the familiar—because standing in front of the
blackboard is Mrs. Wilberton. Ruby Redfort
often says, "There is no greater surprise than the
surprise of the familiar"—like when Ruby
Redfort went camping one time in Peru, and she got
the nasty shock of bumping into her school
archenemy, Vapona Bugwart.

Betty and me look at each other utterly aghast
and bemused because what on earth is she doing
here? She is meant to be on sabbatical—which
means having a term off from teaching because she
has been doing it so long.

It doesn't take long to find out what's gone wrong,
because as soon as she can get her breath, she starts
honking on about what has happened and how

Miss Meyer who is now Mrs. Kelp has got this husband who has got an offer of a good job in Hong Kong and how at the last minute they decided to go and who can blame her—except I can because I am utterly fed up about it. And how can she be so cruel? This is a typical example of grown-ups doing exactly what *they* want to do, not even thinking about the effect it has on other people.

I am completely caught up in my own despair of the situation and I can only just slightly hear Mrs. Wilberton going on about how marvelous she is for canceling her walking-up-the-Alps tour in Switzerland so we won't be without a teacher. And all I can hear is,

"Drone drone drone—*sacrificing my trip*—drone drone drone—*come to the rescue*—drone—*lucky you*—drone drone—*foreseeable future*—drone . . ."

I can't say this is THE WORST WORRY I DIDN'T EVEN THINK TO WORRY ABOUT because to tell you the truth, I do sometimes have a recurring dream where Mrs. Wilberton has moved in with us and I end up sharing a room with her instead of Minal. And when I wake up, I am relieved to see him.

Betty and me are quite downcast, but when it is time to go home, there is call-me-Mol—she is back and standing next to call-me-Cecil. They are smiling like mad and are definitely no longer getting a divorce—which I can tell because they have their arms around each other and they look more pleased about each other than usual.

"It's all in the body language," as Ruby Redfort would say. It's strange, though, because Cecil and Mol not getting a divorce doesn't seem to have cheered Betty up. Maybe she is too depressed about Mrs. Wilberton staying on or maybe she is worrying that Cecil and Mol are going to have another child and that she will have to share a room with it. If this is the worry, then I do *utterly* understand.

The only thing that can cheer me up after such a disastrous first day of school is drama workshop. Betty can't come because she has to go and celebrate Mol getting back from whatever it was she was doing.

Drama workshop is exceptionordinarily interesting and I feel like I am being much more freed up and utterly expressing myself.

I tell Czarina about the **Run, Ruby, Run**
premiere and she is very impressed and is wanting to
make an announcement to the whole of the class but
I say it is top secret and Betty Moody must not find
out and Czarina says, "Darlink, it will not pass my
lips." Which makes me look at her mouth, which is a
strangeish pink due to her nonstop nibbling of beets.

On my way home, I have a very good idea for a
possible twist—Czarina would say this is because my
subconscious has released my creativity. And perhaps
I am being more *avant-garde*.

The second I get in, I scrabble about in my bag
for a piece of paper and I perch on the stairs and
write it down.

Mom is sitting in the kitchen, talking on the
telephone to someone—who knows who, probably
Suki. I am busy writing away and then my ears pick
up the odd word and start to be distracted.

I have acute hearing, which is partly due to my
RUBY REDFORT SPY GUIDE spy training and
partly due to being a middleish child and liking to
know what's going on. She is laughing and saying,

"You're right—if we don't do it *now*, when *will* we? *Yes,* we have *definitely* decided. . . . It will be *quite* an upheaval after all these years. . . . *I know,* it will be so nice to have more *space* . . . and *two* bathrooms. . . . Haven't told the children yet; we'll tell them tomorrow. . . ."

And then I know what the nagging feeling is in the back of my mind—the one I couldn't put my finger on. . . . It must be the WORST WORRY— THE WORST WORRY YOU NEVER EVEN THINK TO WORRY ABOUT.

Moving.

By bedtime my worry has grown even bigger and it is definitely not helping to write it down in my Worst Worry Notebook.

It looks worse somehow—maybe it's because I only had a red pen and it looks more serious in red.

How long is it possible not to Sleep for without collapsing from No Sleep?

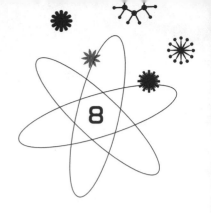

That night I lie in bed worrying like crazy.

If only I was Ruby Redfort, I would think of a plan to stop this happening.

Like the plan Ruby came up with when her mom and dad were trying to move and of course Ruby Redfort utterly cannot move because of HQ being just around the corner, which is her secret agent headquarters and she needs to be near her work at all times and cannot leave Twinford.

What she did was, every time someone came to see if they wanted to buy the house, Ruby would do something to put them off,
i.e., she put bugs and creepy-crawlies in all the kitchen drawers and she borrowed a couple of nonpoisonous snakes from a friend called Flannery

Barklet and she let them loose in the garden—and of course, when the house viewers spotted them they were very off put and said, "Oh my gosh, there are reptiles loose in the yard,"
and Ruby said in her cool-as-a-cucumber way,

"YIKES! They must have
escaped from Mr. Pritchard's
again. . . ."

And Mr. and Mrs. Redfort are always *utterly* confused why people are always rushing out of their house in an utter hurry.

And no one, no one at all, wanted to buy the place even though it is this very super-modern house with an ice dispenser and a remote-control garage, which *anyone* would love.

I will think about trying to do this plan—but I am not sure where to get a large enough snake.

That night I spend many hours trying to nod off— I even do what my dad does when he can't sleep, which is put on a bathrobe and, these days, shoes (due to dust) and sit in a chair on the landing trying to read the paper. I don't find this very helpful because I don't find the paper very interesting.

It mainly seems to be about describing things that have happened in sports or about people caught up in things they wish they hadn't been caught up in. Finally I find a story about how all the polar bears will be soon extinct due to global warming.

Because they say that the earth is getting hotter due to pollution and this is causing the ice to melt in the Arctic, where the polar bears live. And the polar bears might be really good swimmers but they also need somewhere on the land—which is ice— to walk about on and dig a hole, so they can sleep and things.

After 33 minutes I go back to bed—even more tired and much more worried. Minal is snoring away in the next bed and I find myself thinking, as much as I would rather not meet a polar bear because he might be tempted to eat my liver, I also think it would be a very sad thing if they were extinct.

And now I am worrying about
WORRY no.2: strange things
happening to the environment.
Finally I fall asleep wondering how long it is possible not to sleep for without collapsing from no sleep.

In the morning I am a bit woozy and my eyes feel like they have been pressed into my head like raisins.

I am meandering to school thinking about how I will ever tell Betty Moody about us moving—maybe I should tell her about the **Run, Ruby, Run** premiere at the same time—that way I could say what Ruby Redfort always says in this sort of situation: "Should I start with the good news or the bad news?"

And I am also thinking what our new house might be like and will it have stairs, because I like stairs, and then I am thinking about things such as who invented stairs and was it just one person or did lots of people all have the same idea at the same time. And even people in ancient times had stairs so it is a very early invention.

And what would have happened if no one had invented them? Everyone would just have had to wait around until someone invented the elevator.

Then, just as I get to the corner of my road, I remember I have forgotten my math book and I have to run back home and shout through the mail slot because no one is hearing my knocking and our bell is still broken—which it has been for about 5 at least years.

When I finally get in, I can't find my book and so I shout at Mom,
"Where is it?
I bet you have tidied it up somewhere,"
and she shouts back, *"Well, if you ask me, it is probably where you left it, i.e., still in your schoolbag."*
And she is right, which is annoying since she is nearly always right.

And I am feeling annoyed with her anyway about us moving and her being right just makes me more annoyed. And then I have to race out of the house like a maniac and there is no time for meandering and I am not going to be early,

I am going to be mainly most probably late.

Should I start with the Good News or the Bad News?

9

Of course when I get to school, it is more like a usualish day than you could ever imagine.

Mrs. Wilberton says, "Clarice Bean, you are LATE."

And I say, "I know."

And she says, "I will have to put you on the roll as LATE."

And I say, "I know."

And she says, "Any more being LATE for school and you will be staying behind."

And I say, "I know."

And she says, "If you know you will be in trouble for being LATE, then why do you persist in being LATE?"

And I say, "I don't know."

And she says, "Oh, for goodness' sake, go and sit down before you make the whole lesson LATE."

Which is not fair since she is the one who is going on about LATEness.

And if she just wrote me down as LATE, we could all get on with it. She is a typical example of a person who wastes time telling people they are wasting time.

School, as you may know, is not my most favorite thing, and generally I could do without it.

And now I am not sleeping hardly at all—I am finding school more trickier than ever. Betty Moody seems very in the dumps too, and I decide not to tell her about my WORST WORRY, THE WORRY I DIDN'T EVEN THINK TO WORRY ABOUT, because I don't want to make her feel worse.

In assembly Mr. Pickering announces the old persons' center visit—it will happen just before Christmas—and even then Betty doesn't seem excited. And when I say, "I've already put our names down," she just nods without smiling— which *isn't like her.*

Normally she would be very excited by something like this.

Maybe she is coming down with a virus.

There are a lot of them about these days due to all kinds of things which are happening with pollution. Which is of course

WORRY no. 2: strange things happening to the environment.

When we are walking home over the hill, it is almost exactly on the tip of my tongue to tell her my secret about the Ruby Redfort premiere, but luckily just at that moment, Betty whispers, "Don't look now, but look who it is." Who it is, is Justin Broach, and from up here on the hill we can see him coming around the corner of Sesame Park Road just at the same time as this other person is going around the corner the other way—it looks like that boy who sits at the back of our class, called Benji Murtle—he's eating a bag of chips. Betty and I look at each other because we know this means certain doom for Benji Murtle. You never want to bump into Justin Broach by accident

or on purpose—especially when you are eating a bag
of chips.

I think about something Ruby Redfort says in
her **SURVIVAL HANDBOOK**, under
HOW TO AVOID LARGE PREDATORS: "NEVER GET
BETWEEN A LION AND HIS LUNCH."

When I say good-bye to Betty, I don't go exactly
straight home—I sort of meander because I am not
in a hurry to hear the bad news about moving and
where we are going.

I think—what if we end up next door to Justin
Broach? Or perhaps in another place nowhere near
here, in the middle of nowhere.

When I get in, Mom and Dad are both standing
in the kitchen. They look like they are waiting for
something.

My mouth has gone a bit dry.

Mom says, "We've got some exciting news."

I get a creeping cold sensation up my arms and
I wish I was still wearing my coat.

Dad looks at Mom and says, "Where's Kurt?"

Marcie says, "He's with his new drip girlfriend,
Saffron."

Mom says, "I thought he was going out with Jasmine."

Dad says, "I thought she was called Chloe."

I just wish he would just say the bad news—he might as well get it over with.

Marcie says, "*Saffron, Jasmine, Chloe* . . . What's the difference?"

Dad says, "What do you mean?"

Marcie says, "They're all *drips*."

I am thinking—it is probably much worse than I think. They will probably say we will be moving away to a place where we don't even know anyone—in the countryside near probably just some cows. . . . I am looking up at the ceiling wishing this wasn't happening, and as I am wishing this, I realize I am hearing Dad saying, ". . . and Clarice will be moved into the attic."

It takes me a few moments of thinking to realize what he is talking about and then I can hardly breathe because I am stunned with relief.

I can't believe it, my WORST WORRY— THE WORRY I DIDN'T EVEN THINK TO WORRY ABOUT is not my worst worry after all—

everything is going to be all right—

we are not moving away—

instead the house is being
mended and there will be another actual bathroom
and more space and I am going to be moved into
the attic, which will become my own actual room.

I want to be moved into the attic.

I really do.

Except for one thing.

WORRY no. 9: largish spiders.

As much as I like the idea of being in an attic
I am concerned about the number of largish spiders
that I have seen up there.

I don't want to say anything out loud about this
problem in case Mom and Dad change their minds,
so I write it down in my notebook and hope,
as Ruby would say, that "The solution will just
come to me."

How to Know Things without Knowing Things

Of course, I wake up in an exceptionordinarily good mood. And all my worst worries seem far away—even infinity seems a long way off.

I leave for school extra early so I can tell Betty about the room of my own before school starts—I am actually running along and I even shout *hello* at Robert Granger as I nip past him.

Unfortunately, as I run along Sesame Park Road, I spot Justin Broach. He is emptying rubbish from the can all over the pavement—his friend, the boy with the odd haircut, is laughing. I don't feel like walking past them, which means I have to go all around the back of Sydney Street. Which means I will be late. When I get into class, there is no sign of Betty—and then I remember how she was a bit off-color yesterday and how she is probably having to take the day off from school due to illness. Mrs. Wilberton tells me off for lateness of course and says I will be kept behind after school—but I don't even mind because I am distracted by my good fortune.

And when the bell rings, I walk out of class and there is Betty Moody.

I say, "Betty, I thought you were off being ill."

She says, "No, I am just late because I had to talk to Mr. Pickering."

And I think that's funny because Betty Moody is never in trouble—she never has to go and see Mr. Pickering but I say, "Oh."

She is not smiling and she is looking down and kind of keeps pulling her socks up.

When they don't need pulling up.

These are all the signs of someone about to tell you some bad news. I learned that from Ruby Redfort.

And it is a very hard thing to lie or have bad news or even good news and not find yourself giving it away.

And there are people like the police or the secret

service who are highly trained to be good at noticing these giveaway signs and it is very difficult to trick them unless you are an expert liar and possibly a criminal.

Betty Moody turns out not to be an expert liar or good at keeping something bad to herself because after quite a lot of standing on one leg and buckling and unbuckling her shoe she says,
"Clarice Bean, I am afraid I have got some really bad news for you."

And I say, "I know."

And she says, "How come?"

And I say, "I have been reading **THE RUBY REDFORT SPY GUIDE: HOW TO KNOW THINGS WITHOUT KNOWING THINGS**."

And she says, "Oh."

And then she says, "Do you mean, you *know* I have some bad news or do you *actually know* what the bad news is?"

And I say, "No, I don't *know* what the bad news is; all I know is that there *is* some."

And she says, "Oh."

And then she doesn't say anything.

And I don't say anything because I don't want to hear it.

And I wish I could just say,

"Don't look now, but look who it is."

Just to sort of distract her—but I can't.

I mean, maybe it won't be that bad.

But she is pulling up her socks again—and I know that it must be.

She says, "Well, you remember when Mol stayed on in California?"

I say, "Yes, on vacation."

And Betty says, "Well, she wasn't on vacation. She was going for an interview for a job—at a university."

I say, "Oh," because you see I still don't get it.

And Betty says, "Well, they offered her the job . . ."

I don't speak.

And Betty says, "And Mol said yes."

I still don't speak.

And Betty says, "So we are moving . . . to San Francisco."

And all of a sudden I feel like something is whooshing in my ears. And I am looking at her socks like crazy.

They are stripy over-the-knee ones and I think
they are new.

I am standing very still and I am thinking,
and I am thinking it's much worse than I thought—
how could it be much more worse than this?

And she says, "We are leaving next week."

And I bite my lip really hard and it starts to bleed.

But I don't care.

Because I don't care about anything now.

She says, "I am really sorry, Clarice Bean."

But I can't say anything.

Lots of thoughts are whirring about in my mind,
but I am not sure what any of them are because
they are not stopping; they are just whirring.

And Betty touches my arm and says,
"It will be OK, CB. We can write."

And I say, "*Yep.*"

And I can't say more than *yep,*
because my voice won't say more than *yep,*
and what I really want—is to go home.

What Ruby would say about this is,
"You just gotta take it on the chin."

That's what she says about most things but then

she has never had her *utterly best friend* move to San Francisco—and even if this did happen, she has always got her purple helicopter.

I walk back from school on my own because Mrs. Wilberton makes me stay behind for lateness but I don't care because I don't want to be with anyone—not even Betty.

Sometimes there is no Twist

Tomorrow is the day of Betty leaving and I am not being able to think about much else. Every morning it is the very first thing I think about and when I drop off to sleep at night, it is the last thing I know. My mind can't stop itself—it is the only thought it has going on.

And I spend quite a lot of minutes looking out of the window and watching the rain trickle down the glass. It is fascinating in a boring kind of way.

It's boring because it reminds me of being bored on car trips and also at school and also of weekends where there is nothing to do.

I have spent lots of minutes watching rain trickle down windows so I know how it goes and how it is not always a straight line. The rain sort of wiggles but none of this surprises me, because I know rain always wiggles.

I go over to the Moodys' to say good-bye.

There are Mol and Cecil and Betty, and we all take photographs of each other and we all are being nice and laughing but in a strange way. And Cecil and Mol and Betty look the same—look like themselves but at the same time different. Sort of like they aren't really there.

Betty gives me her beanbag—she says that way I will have two. And she says I can keep her **RUBY REDFORT SPY GUIDE: HOW TO KNOW THINGS WITHOUT KNOWING THINGS**.

And I give her the Macey Gruber story I have been writing—it's sort of finished except for the end— I never know how to do the end.

And you see, there is no twist and I say good-bye.

And just like that Betty Moody is gone.

So now perhaps you can see that Ruby Redfort is right—that your worst worry is the worry you haven't even thought to worry about. And it is difficult to see it coming. You may just feel it creeping up on you, but you won't know what it is, because how can you imagine the unimaginable if you can't imagine it?

And I sit there thinking about **Run, Ruby, Run** and I realize I didn't even get a chance to tell Betty that she was invited to the best thing she has probably ever been invited to. And I will never get the chance to say, "Don't look now, but we are standing next to Skyler Summer."

Now I will have to go on my own, alone.

It's just been raining and raining, and when Grandad and Cement come back from their walk, they look sort of flattish.

Like the rain has battered them down.

I am sitting at the kitchen table trying to think what I should write for my *"All about me"* homework.

I can't think of anything.

Nothing.

You see I don't feel like me anymore.

So I have nothing to say.

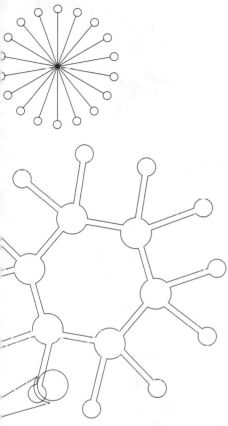

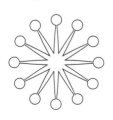

PART TWO

The Same but Not the Same

What to do
when you are
Lost at Sea

I wake up from a bad dream. In it, everyone at
school ganged up against me and even Betty Moody
was ignoring me and suddenly I had no friends. And
the dream gives me this funny feeling like something
has actually really happened and it takes me a while to
tell myself that it is all not true—that Betty Moody
did not ignore me in school, because I haven't been
in school—I have been asleep, sleeping.

And everything is really all right.

And that's when I remember what I have been
trying to forget:

That everything is not all right.

Because you see something bad has happened that
is much worse than in my dream.

Betty Moody has gone.

Someone ignoring you is not so dreadful because you can make that right.

But if someone isn't there at all . . . it doesn't matter what is right and what is wrong because they aren't there either way.

THE RUBY REDFORT SURVIVAL HANDBOOK is on the floor next to my bed, and I pick it up and start reading a new bit called WHAT TO DO IF YOU ARE MAROONED AT SEA.

Ruby could see that her tiny yacht was fast taking on water. In a snap she had inflated her survival dinghy, grabbed the last of her precious drinking water, and jumped aboard. She'd made it—just in time to see her trusty boat sink to the inky depths of the deep gray ocean.

What to do in this situation?
First of all, do not panic and do not start crazily paddling. Conserve your energy— in other words, stay still—until you get your bearings. Then look for DRY LAND. You will only survive on your own for so long— you MUST find the shore and human life.

I am beginning to wonder how all this Ruby
Redfort advice is of any use to me, Clarice Bean,
schoolgirl. I have never been marooned at sea
and it is unlikely that I will be, since I avoid boats
due to seasickness.

I am just putting the book back on the shelf
by my bed when I see the red envelope—
the one containing the special tickets to the movie of
Run, Ruby, Run.

I go up to my new attic room—it is just a space.
When I walk in, there is a creaking sound and
one of the floorboards seems a bit springy—
it isn't nailed down properly.

I kneel on my knees and I find I can lift it up—
it is not attached. There is a useful space underneath
where I can keep things. I decide to put my
Run, Ruby, Run tickets in the gap.

I suppose I do this mainly because they are so
valuable, but also because part of me doesn't want
to look at them anymore. It's also a good place
to keep my two Ruby handbooks when I am not
reading them—I will be able to get them out

whenever I want. Ruby Redfort is always hiding important things just to be on the safe side.

I am thinking about Betty Moody leaving and how I never would have thought it was possible and that this is truly the worst thing that has ever happened to me. And then I think now that the worst thing has happened at least that is that— I don't need to worry anymore.

But as I am thinking about this, it dawns on me that there is always a worse thing that can happen. Because now that the worst thing has happened, it means the second-to-worst thing can happen and that will be the new worst thing and there is always a worry you have never thought to worry about.

There is always *something*
worse than your
worst, worst
worry.

What to do when you are confronted by Alien Life-Forms

13

At 8 a.m. on the dot, the builders arrive and they take their shoes off when they come in—which Mom likes even though the floor is more dirty than their shoes.

The builders (who are Polish) say the work will take two months—which Dad says means at least three and most probably four. . . . "In fact we might as well order an extra big turkey for Christmas because they will be almost family by then."

I am not a morning person and I am finding the noise of lots of men walking about in our house very disagreeable. Also Mom has been moving things from one place to another completely different one and I can't find a single pair of socks or even two single socks not in a pair. I end up going into

Marcie's room to borrow some of hers and she catches me at it.

She says, "What are you doing in my room, brat? Get out before I count to ten or you will wish you had."

Mom hears Marcie's screeching and calls out,

"Marce, can I have a word?"

And I know what she will be saying. She will be saying, "Do you think you could be a little nicer to your sister because she has just had an utterly best friend desert her forever, whom she will never see again as long as she lives probably and she is not feeling her level best"— something like that, anyway.

I end up wearing a pair of Kurt's socks to school, which means my shoes don't fit properly since his feet are much bigger than mine and the heel bit is halfway up my leg almost.

It makes it very difficult to walk, particularly because it's a very blowy day and this just adds to my problems.

When I get to school, there is this new girl.

She is pretty—prettier than me.

She has this blond hair—very whitish blond.

And shiny all over.

My hair is shiny at the front and then all fuzzy at the back where I can't get to it with the brush.

She has pointy green eyes and she is quite brown with long legs.

She doesn't wear the same clothes as anyone at my school—they are just sort of different slightly.

She has on a red skirt with straps and a stripy top. I have never seen anyone who looks like her before except maybe Uncle Ted's girlfriend, Stina, who is from a place called Scandinavia.

Everyone is buzzing around her, like they are wasps.

Karl is acting a bit funny too.

He keeps hanging around and swinging on the pegs. Whenever she speaks, he agrees a lot and smiles like a chimpanzee.

I am wondering what's gone wrong with him.

In assembly, Mr. Pickering announces who the new girl is.

She is called Clem Hansson, and she has come from a place called Stockholm, in Sweden. She is standing next to Mrs. Larch.

Mr. Pickering stops talking and Mrs. Larch makes an announcement about the school pet show. It actually sounds quite interesting and I really like animals and I am thinking maybe I will take part because I can enter Fuzzy, our cat. He is Burmese, which is a special breed—it means he is a bit like a dog and will come when he's called and he is more friendly than other cats because he is not very cat-ish. People always like Fuzzy so all I have to do is make sure he is very groomed. If Betty Moody was still here, she would have entered her dog, Ralph, but she isn't. I am in a slight daydream and I hardly hear Mrs. Wilberton saying, "*Clarice Bean,* would you come over here for a minute?"

I can't believe it because I am not late or anything today.

Mrs. Wilberton is standing there with the new girl and what she says is,
"Clarice, I was thinking because Betty Moody has now left us, you will be free to look after Clem Hansson and make sure she knows just where everything is in the school and how we like to go about things. You can start by showing her the toilets," and suddenly I am having

WORRY no. 10: having to talk to people you don't know and don't want to know.

The new girl is looking at me and not smiling— she doesn't say anything but she is waiting for me to say something.

So I say, "Follow me" and I walk off—she is sort of scurrying behind me, trying to keep up—I can be quite a fast walker when I want to be. When we get to the toilets, I say, "Those are the toilets." You would have to be really stupid indeed not to know they were the toilets because they say TOILETS on the door and there is a sign of a person in a dress which means toilet as everybody well knows.

In class Mrs. Wilberton has put the new girl next to me—in *Betty's seat*.

I notice she has taken all her pens out of her pencil case—which is in fact not a case but a wooden box. She has laid them all out on the table like a rainbow.

She has a lot of pens.

There's something about her I don't like.

When Mrs. Wilberton asks her to tell everyone about herself, she stands there like she can't be bothered almost and she says about her dad getting a job over here and that hopefully they might go back to Sweden one day and she says she has a rabbit and *he is Swedish too.*

And afterward, at recess, she follows me out into the playground, but she doesn't say one thing to me. And then Karl comes up and says, "My brother has a rabbit." And I think, What's happening? Why is everybody talking about rabbits all of a sudden? All they do is nibble and hop about, and out of the corner of my eye I can see Justin Broach lurking around, and he's looking at the new girl too.

Then all these other people from my class all come over and start asking her things.

She says, "My father is Swedish and my mother is Swedish but my mother's best friend is English and that's why I am called Clem—after her," and Grace Grapello says, "What's Sweden like?" and Clem says, "It is the best place to live because there is lots to do and you can go skiing and we have a summerhouse over there."

I feel as if some creatures from outer space, who want to take over the world in the usual way creatures from outer space do, have come and sprayed everyone with a mystery solution and it is making everybody behave all really peculiarly so that I am the only normal one—only I feel like the only weird one because I am now the odd one out. It reminds me of this bit in **THE RUBY REDFORT SURVIVAL HANDBOOK** called WHAT TO DO WHEN YOU ARE CONFRONTED BY ALIEN LIFE-FORMS.

Ruby wasn't sure at first, but there was something strange about the way Mrs. Hasselberg was drinking her coffee. Whenever she raised her cup to take a sip, she sort of dangled her finger in her drink, which seemed to cause an alarming gurgling sound. Ruby couldn't be 100 percent sure, but she suspected that Mrs. Hasselberg might be drinking cappuccino through her index finger.

It is very disconcerting to find yourself face-to-face with someone not of your species. What to do: First, you must ascertain if they are friend or foe. This can be difficult—remember, they may not understand your customs or greetings. A smile and a handshake may be considered highly aggressive actions and may be mistaken for baring of teeth and grabbing of limb—or in some cases, tentacle. Try to keep a respectful distance and not stare. If it transpires that the alien in question is a foe, act as if you are unaware of its hostile status—i.e., just play along—and when the moment allows, give it the slip and run like crazy.

WARNING: ALIENS OFTEN HAVE CONCEALED ZAPPERS.

Everyone in my school seems really interested in Clem Hansson, like she has come from Mars when in fact it is only Sweden.

I sort of wander off on my own because the thing is I don't really feel like talking to anyone,

     not even

       someone

         from   Mars.

Getting Tangled in your own Lasso

When I get back home, I want not to be noticed but that is very hard at the moment because there are seven people in my family and there are practically no rooms that aren't filled with rubble or no furniture—so everyone has to be crowded into one space.

I do sometimes wish I could go invisible and then at least no one would talk to me when I didn't want them to. There's this brilliant bit in **THE RUBY REDFORT SPY GUIDE** about her getting this invisibility jumpsuit and she manages to go to all these very interesting places where you are not usually let in and suddenly you are a bit like a fly on a wall.

And flies on walls get to hear everything.

If they have ears, that is. . . .

Do flies have ears?

Before suppertime, I creep up to the attic room—
my almost room—even though it's unfinished
and smells of dead mice, I find I like being up there
because it is warm and quietish—apart from the
gurgling of the hot-water pipes. I read a bit from
THE RUBY REDFORT SPY GUIDE—it's a
chapter called HOW TO FAKE IT. She teaches you
how to fake anything from extreme illness to
speaking a foreign language.

I think I will fake a mildish illness that requires
staying home from school.

When I go downstairs for supper, I see it is
another toast-based dish.

I decide to go to bed early without dinner because
A, I don't feel like having to talk to anyone and B,
I am sick of toast.

Later that evening Mom comes into my room—
she wants to know what is wrong. I make up a bit of
a fib about a headacheish tummyache that is causing
my limbs to feel a bit detached. I think it is better to
not have just one symptom because I am not sure

what is the best thing to be wrong with me, but I get lucky because Mom says, "*Mmm, could be flu.*" As you may know, I am quite a good actor now so I manage to do a small sigh and say,
"*Oh no, do you think?*"

She puts her hand on my head. I dampened it with a wet, cold washcloth before she came in— I learned that from Ruby.

Anyway, the effect of a dampened washcloth on the forehead makes you seem a bit feverish.

Mom says, "Clarice darling, I think you may well have to stay home tomorrow."

I make a slight groaning sound—this is a good touch and suggests a disappointment and eagerness not to miss a smidge of school. Parents like this and are more likely to keep you home if they know you are keen on going.

Before she turns out the light, she says, "Who will you take to the **Run, Ruby, Run** premiere?" and I say, "No one, I don't think" and she says, "Oh you must take *someone*. How about Karl?" and I say,
"He goes back to see his cousins in Ireland at

Christmas." And she says, "Oh . . . Well, I am sure we can think of someone" and I think, What's the point of taking anyone? No one understands Ruby Redfort like Betty Moody does.

That night I hardly sleep at all, which is a relief because when I am asleep, I find myself dreaming dreadful dreams. One is about the **Run, Ruby, Run** premiere and because I can't think of anyone to take with me, Mom invites Justin Broach, who gives Skyler Summer a Chinese burn.

In the morning, Mom comes in and takes a look at me—I can tell I don't look that good because she puts her head on one side and makes a tutting sound. I am not even putting it on—it must be the no sleep that is causing me to look dreadfully wretched.

Mom says, "You had better stay home."

I groan.

Mom says, "I will go and make a few calls to see if I can get off work."

I groan.

Mom goes off to make her calls and I stare up at the crack in the ceiling—I think it is getting bigger.

While I am lying there, I remember what Ruby Redfort always says about faking illness: "Never get too confident—if you are pretending to be sick, then act sick."

Mom comes back a few minutes later and says, "I am afraid I couldn't get off work because several people have phoned in sick.
But luckily Mrs. Hibbert has kindly said she can come over."

I really groan. This is very bad news because although Mrs. Hibbert is a very nice person, she just never stops talking. And so it means I will either have to pretend to be asleep all day or I will have to listen to her talking about her grown-up son and daughter who have both ended up moving to New Zealand for some reason.

I quickly change my mind about staying home and say, "You know what? I am fine really; I will go to school."

And Mom says, "No, you are not going to school, *uh-uh*—you look terrible."

And I say, "What about the builders? They can keep an eye on me; they are just downstairs."

Mom just looks at me as if I am delirious and says Mrs. Hibbert will be here in twenty minutes.

This is what Ruby Redfort would call "getting tangled in your own lasso." Unfortunately, I have been too good at faking it and am now stuck with Mrs. Hibbert for the day.

I wish Betty Moody was around—she would know what to do; she would probably say, "Don't look now, but I've got an idea." If I could even e-mail her, that would be something, but she did say it would take a couple of weeks before her Internet thingy would be set up.

The hours pass quite incredibly slowly. One thing I start to think is why doesn't Ruby Redfort have a page on how to get out of boring conversations and dreary days—like when you have to go visit people you don't really know and sit around talking to their children *just because they are children too,* and you are supposed to get along with them but why? And thinking about this makes me think of my `WORRY no. 8: being bored to nearly utter death`. It's in my `Worst Worry Notebook`—I thought of it last summer when we had to visit a family called the Stevenses.

By the time it is twelve minutes past five o'clock, I have seen 76 photographs of Mrs. Hibbert's children, Michael and Susan, and I know that:

Susan is thinking about having another baby but is worried about whether she wants to give up her job at the bank which she loves because everyone is so friendly and pleasant and aren't just work people but more than that they are the kind of people you can enjoy seeing for a light supper too. Michael fell off a boat when he was fishing last Easter and he is quite frankly lucky to be here what with the dangerous currents and whatnot mind you he was back on the ocean the following weekend because you can't let a brush with death stop you doing what you want to do.

After listening to Mrs. Hibbert for 9 hours I am thinking I might upgrade `WORRY no. 8: being bored to nearly utter death` to `WORRY`

no. 6, because you see being bored to nearly utter
death is a very serious problem and can be quite
dangerous because it saps you of all your energy,
and the more bored you get, the more you aren't
able to do anything to stop yourself from being bored.

Ruby would say,

"When this happens, you just gotta get a grip."

At 6 o'clock I am very relieved to see Mom home
and I tell her I am feeling much better thank you
and I am *definitely* going to school tomorrow even if
my leg has dropped off.

Mom also looks very relieved to hear this as she
still can't get out of work because Mr. Larsson is
causing all the workers at the old persons' center to
call in sick—at least that is what Mom thinks.

She says, "I mean how else do you explain *three
separate cases* of food poisoning—*coincidence?*
I don't think so—more like they don't want to
have to break up a fight between two pensioners."

As it turns out, Mr. Larsson has been sitting in
Mrs. Flemming's chair and Mom says, "Mrs.
Flemming isn't one to take this lying down."

After tea, Mom says she has got something for me.

It turns out to be a new pair of shoes—they are brown suede and slightly more like boots than shoes in fact, and they have red laces. They're nice and they are like the ones that Cecil and Mol got for Betty Moody.

When I put them on, Mom is looking at me in this over-keenish way to see my reaction. Looking at my feet in them makes me feel sad because they remind me of Betty, but I keep that inside—I don't want her to see, and so I try my best to look extremely delighted, but I am not sure she is convinced.

Ruby says, "Faking looking happy when you are given a present is one of the hardest things to do."

Mom sort of bites her lip and her eyebrows meet in this sad way. And I feel bad because you see she is wanting to cheer me up and make me feel better.

But I won't let her.

How to Survive in Shark-Infested Waters

15

My not-sleeping has been getting worse and I am not sleeping most of the night. And I am finding it hard to do my writing because I no longer have my Ruby flashlight—so I have no way of uncluttering my mind of all the buzzing thoughts.

I am like a walking zombie because 4 hours' sleep or even five is not enough for most normal human people. I looked it up on the computer and it said most people need 8 hours' sleep per night and that not having enough sleep can make you not so clever because your brain is not refreshed and so it cannot store information properly. It can also make it very hard to make good decisions.

It's true because a good decision the next morning would be not to get up at all, maybe not even open my eyes.

Since when I do open my eyes, the first thing I see is my brother Minal.

He is on the floor arranging his collection of plastic insects.

It's amazing how interesting he can find this.

Minal sleeps for hours and hours without ever waking up once with worry—so it is surprising he is not a more intelligent life-form.

I manage to step on a plastic millipede, which really hurts, and so I have to hobble downstairs on mainly one leg.

The hall is full of Polish builders who are all drilling and pulling bits off the wall. It is quite noisy and not at all pleasant for someone with a headache due to lack of sleep.

Mom is at the bottom of the stairs staring at Dad with her hands on her hips—this way of standing means she has asked him a question which isn't really a question, i.e., will you be back by seven? And Dad is saying, "Yes, I will be back by 7." He has learned that this body language of Mom's means—*whatever you do, make sure it is agreeing.* And Ruby Redfort would agree with Dad about agreeing with Mom because she says, **"It is vital for a spy's survival that he or she read the signs."**

And of course you don't need to be a spy to need survival.

Mom says, "Good, because I have to go in and deal with Mr. Larsson today, so I will be utterly at my wits' end by this evening and I would appreciate some help from you."

Dad says, "You got it, OK," and then he kisses her good-bye.

When Mom sees me, she says, "Are you feeling better? You still look a little pale."

And I say, "I think it is just from lack of sunlight— I will look more colorful when I get outside."

And Mom says, "Mmm, well, make sure you have some breakfast."

Someone has finished all the Sugar Puffs (they aren't actually Sugar Puffs—they are just puffs, because Mom is worried that we are all addicted to sugary things).

I have some slightly stale Rice Krispies, which are not krispie at all.

And I am off—quite fast—to school because I do not want to be staying behind for lateness.

I get there early, which is a miracle since my new shoelaces keep coming undone and I have to keep stopping to do them up every 5 minutes. But anyway, now that there is no Betty, there is no point being there early because even though I do have other friends, they are used to talking to the people they always talk to and it is hard to just join in with someone else.

I can see Clem in the playground, she looks up when I walk past, she is being surrounded by Grace Grapello.

I don't know why Clem wants to be friends with her and Cindy Fisher so much—but if she does, that's fine with me. I can hear her going on and on about Sweden. Out of the corner of my eye I see Justin Broach and the boy with the odd haircut moving over to where Clem is standing.

If she was sensible she would nip off while she still has the chance but I expect she will be making friends with them next.

I sit down on the bench under the tree. It's the

one near the bike sheds—hardly anyone usually sits over here.

I read a section of Ruby Redfort called HOW TO SURVIVE IN SHARK-INFESTED WATERS. Ruby explains what to do if you should have the unfortunate misfortune to fall off your boat while sailing in a sea full of sharks.

The main thing to do is not have a cut oozing blood.

Nor must you pee in the water.

Sharks *love* this.

Although, if they do, they should try coming to our local swimming pool—Robert Granger is always peeing in the water and his wart bandage nearly always comes off and floats about in the pool.

Once my brother Minal almost swallowed it.

Anyway, if you can avoid these two no-no's, then the next thing to do is not to swim away from a shark when it is swimming toward you. It might sound like utterly madness to the non-expert, but what you should do is, strangely, "Swim toward it."

This puts them off because they stop thinking you are something to nibble on—plus they aren't as confident as they like to think they are and in fact are a little bit nervous of things swimming toward them.

It helps if you have a big stick.

Ruby says, "Whatever you do, do not let them explore you with their teeth." They like to do this—this is a shark's way of getting to know you, but their teeth are awfully sharp and can cause a lot of damage. And just a nip from a shark might mean waving good-bye to your arm.

Clem Hansson has brought a tin of homemade cookies to school. They are sort of gingery and decorated.

I am astonished to see her go up to Justin Broach and the boy with the odd haircut and offer them one. In fact she offers them to everyone—everyone except *me*, but maybe she doesn't see me. I am beginning to turn invisible.

By lunchtime, I wish I was wearing my raincoat because even though the weather has turned all drizzly, we still have to go outside after lunch, although I notice that Justin Broach and the boy with the odd haircut manage to sneak back into the coatrooms when no one is looking. I am noticing all kinds of things since I am spending more time on my own. Noah and Suzie Woo and people keep asking me to hang out with them but I am just not in the mood. And I am not going to hang out with Karl because he is usually messing around with Toby Hawkling, and Toby Hawkling can be very annoying. It's hard to read my book on the bench in the drizzle without it getting damp and it's difficult to concentrate.

I have just finished a bit about what to do when you have been bitten by a highly venomous snake, when something makes me look up and I see Clem Hansson staring at me across the playground. She is looking at me in a strange way—like she might be wondering what I am reading because you see I am always reading and I don't think she likes it that I am more interested in Ruby Redfort, who is a book character, than in her, who is a real actual person.

In the afternoon, Mrs. Wilberton asks Clem Hansson why she has forgotten her gym clothes. And she says she hasn't forgotten them because she is sure they were hanging on her peg earlier before lunch break, and Mrs. Wilberton just says, "Well, in normal circumstances I would be a little angry but since you are new, I will make an exception." This is utterly not fair and I don't see why she shouldn't get told off since everybody else does—all the time.

I am hanging around by the pegs trying to find my gloves and I hear Karl say to Clem Hansson, "I heard we will soon be getting our new permanent teacher—hopefully one without trotters."

Clem Hansson looks at him in a blankish way because it turns out that maybe they don't have trotters in Scandinavia. Then Karl does his trotter impression and she thinks this is very funny and I realize it is the first time I have seen her laugh.

I am walking home and thinking about when he first did this joke for me—to cheer me up—and how it is our joke, and why is he doing it for other people?

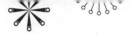

When you get to the End of your Rope — let go

16

The next day turns out to be one of those nothing days where nothing much happens and even the weather is that nothing weather—just grayness. Clem has come to school wearing this stripy bobble hat. It's mainly red and it has a long point so that the bobble hangs right down her back.

It's a bit like something a pixie would wear. When she runs, the bobble sort of bounces. And you can easily see who she is on the playground.

At recess on my way to the bench, I overhear her telling some people that she was given it by her grandmother—who knitted it herself.

And I hear Cindy Fisher say, "It is really nice. Does she knit other things like sweaters and scarves, or does she only do hats?"

And Clem says, "Well, she has died now and this is the only thing I have left that she knitted for me."

And Suzie Woo says, "Oh." And then Karl says, "I still have one grandmother left; she lives in Ireland."

Justin Broach is standing around but he doesn't say anything—he just listens.

At the end of the day I go to collect my coat from my peg and I notice Clem Hansson standing right next to it. And I wonder what she is up to because her peg is nowhere near my peg—it's on the other side of the coatroom.

On my way out from school, I see the notice board. Mr. Pickering has put a list up of all the people who have volunteered for the old persons' center visit. Betty Moody's name has been scratched out and my name is the only one not in a pair.

I am wondering what Betty Moody is doing.

I am still waiting for her to e-mail me. I have been checking in the school library. Karl comes up to me and asks if I would like to go swimming with him and Alf. They are going to the rec center, where there is a pool that has waves. They are pretend, made by machine. I would really like to go but I say, "I have to go to drama workshop tonight," which in fact I am looking forward to—it's just I would rather not go on my own.

I say to Karl, "Do you think you might want to sign up to visit the old persons' center and do the thing of making an old person a cup of tea and having a chat?"

Karl says he has nothing against old people and he doesn't mind being friends with anyone, but he doesn't want to be *told* to talk to somebody. He says if he just happens to meet a person, then fine, but he doesn't like the whole forcing people to have a cup of tea together.

I do sort of know what he means, but he has to remember that some of the people at the old persons' center don't get out that much, so they don't have the chance to just meet people in a normal way.

Just to make my day even more slightly worse, when I get to drama workshop, there is a notice on the door which says:

Sorry to disappoint, darlinks, but I am afraid I have been advised to cancel drama workshop as I am having a baby and my doctor says I have been overdoing things, don't lose sight of your dreams, and don't let anyone rain on your parade, **Czarina**

Everybody seems to be raining on my parade these days. Even *her.*

Why does she have to go and have a baby now, just when everything else in my actual life is going wrong? And now it is even too late to go swimming with Karl and Alf.

I turn around and guess what? Robert Granger is standing right behind me. This is what can happen if there is no one to say, "Don't look now, but Robert Granger is standing right behind you."

He says, "Drama workshop has been canceled."

I say, "I can read, twit."

And he says, "It's a shame."

I don't say anything because I don't want to encourage him.

I start walking off home and of course he follows.

He is walking in a running kind of way and he just keeps on babbling, and even though I don't say a word back, he just yaks on.

"Clarice Bean, your shoelace is coming undone."

Which it is and it is annoying because it also makes it harder to walk faster—I am beginning to hate these shoes. And I can still hear Robert going, "*Clarice Bean,* I am learning the piano. *Clarice Bean,* what are you doing to your house? *Clarice Bean,* Arnie Singh's got a backpack a bit like that. Did you copy him?"

And my head is almost going crazy with all his babbling and I think to myself, I must read **THE RUBY REDFORT SPY GUIDE** chapter called HOW TO LOSE A TAIL—she means *tail* as in someone tailing you and following you around— not *tail* as in tail of a fox.

Robert Granger is a worst worry who is always

right behind me somewhere. I will write him in my `Worst Worry Notebook` as **`WORRY no. 19:`** `Robert Granger—will he ever leave me alone?`—it's surprising I haven't thought to do this before.

I get home and I absolutely bang the front door shut because Czarina says it is important to express yourself sometimes—even if it is uncomfortable for everyone else. But in fact nobody even notices because the builders are still all over the place bashing walls down.

I wave at Grandad. He has got his hearing aids out because the noise is not at all something that you would want to listen to. He is surrounded by the washing machine and lots of kitchenish things that have been piled up in his room.

He doesn't seem to mind.

I decide to take the pack of Fig Newtons up to my attic room so I can see if it is changed.

When I get up there, I find that the Polish builders are all busy mending the walls. I offer them the cookies, which they are really pleased about as I think they are a bit hungry. They seem extremely nice and I ask the main one who is called Jacek what the word for cookie is in Polish and he says it is "ciastko."

And I decide I think I will learn Polish. He has popped a new window in my attic room because the old one was a bit small and also rotten. Jacek says it is a nice room because it faces southwest and gets the afternoon sun and on clear nights I will be able to see the stars.

The thing is I have gone off the stars a bit because they remind me of infinity and how big the world is and how I can't do anything to stop all the pollution and the litter and I can't stop the ice from melting either—because I am just a tiny speck on the planet.

And however small the stars look to me from my window, I look even smaller to them. If you were trying to look at me from a star or a spaceship, I would be barely minuscule—

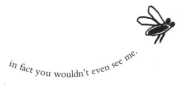

in fact you wouldn't even see me.

Is it possible to be Happy and Sad at the Same Time?

The next day I am woken by the very unusual sound of no noise. I go into the bathroom and the hole in the floor has come back. The builders did cover it up for a while to stop people dropping through, but they must have uncovered it again this morning—but where are they?

When I go down for breakfast, I see that my mother is on the phone. She has it tucked under her chin and she is waving her left arm around like anything and her right hand is pointing at a piece of paper. She is doing a lot of shouting and saying things like, "Either *you* are a moron or *I* am a moron, because I really can't make sense of anything you are saying." My mother has to wave her arms around when she is angry and even though the people at the end of the telephone can't see her, it helps her sound more in charge. Czarina would agree with waving arms because she says we should use our whole bodies to express ourselves and to project our point of view.

Mom is getting far too angry and that is why Dad usually makes these kind of complaint calls because he is good at keeping his cool and sounding reasonable at all times. He always says, "They simply won't listen to you if you sound like a crazy lunatic."

He is right because I find that when Mom is sounding like a crazy lunatic, I usually avoid being in the same room as her.

It turns out she is shouting at Town Hall because they have towed away the Polish builders' van because Town Hall says the Polish builders aren't allowed to park without permission and Mom says they did have permission and Town Hall says it wasn't the right kind of permission. And Mom says, "Surely permission is permission. If I am not already insane now, then I will certainly be by the end of this conversation."

She slams down the phone and then she says,

"Where is your father when I need him? He is supposed to make these phone calls."

Then the phone rings right away again and Mom picks it up on the first ring and says, "*What!* Oh, sorry, Frank. . . . *No,* no, I have just had a tricky morning—that's all. . . . Everything's *fine.* . . . Sure you can. . . . Go ahead, ask me. . . . Yes, I'm free, why? . . . *Mr. Larsson!* Are you sure there isn't anyone else who could take him to the dentist? . . . Really? OK, OK. Bye then, Frank."

Mom slams down the phone. "*Why me?* Is the world trying to *tell me* something? Does the world *hate me?*"

I can tell this is not a good moment to mention whether or not she managed to buy more Snackle Pops, so I just nibble on a half-eaten piece of toast and nip off to school smartish.

Now that I have gotten in the habit of reading my **RUBY REDFORT SURVIVAL HANDBOOK** and my **RUBY REDFORT SPY GUIDE** during recess, I am saved from having to hang around listening to everyone go on about Clem Hansson all the time—which is what they mainly do. Today she is wearing this coat that has lots of pockets with badges stitched onto them and everybody keeps asking if they can try it on.

I am watching her from behind my book and I can see Robert Granger go over and stand next to her. He isn't talking for once but he is smiling and nodding and trying to share his chips with her. She has sort of hypnotized everybody and one by one they are all getting pulled like magnets to be her friends. I don't mind about Robert Granger but I wish she would stop trying to take Karl Wrenbury.

She has even joined gymnastics club—which is most probably because Karl is in it. It is tonight after school and so I see her hanging about with all the gymnastics people. She is talking to Justin Broach while Karl Wrenbury is trying to show off with Toby Hawkling. He is making faces behind Justin Broach's back and he will get a Chinese burn if he is not careful. Lots of my friends do gymnastics but I don't because on gymnastics day Betty and me used to watch Ruby Redfort and come up with ideas.

Also I am not that bendable.

Just as I am walking past Clem, she drops her hat

on the floor almost right in front of me but she doesn't pick it up. And I can't help thinking she is waiting for me to pick it up and I think why? She is just standing right by it. And she is looking at me— not smiling, just waiting, and then Karl Wrenbury bends down and hands it to her. And I think, why can't she pick up her own hat?

When I get home, Kurt is sitting reading a magazine about music. He doesn't look like himself or maybe I mean he looks like his old self, i.e., gloomy. I am a bit nervous to ask but I need to check if Betty Moody might have sent me an e-mail by now—she said by today she would—and Mom has absolutely banned me and Minal from using her laptop because of an orange juice spillage in the keyboard.

I use a Ruby Redfort technique from her **SPY GUIDE** which she explains in a chapter called GETTING WHAT YOU WANT—THE ART OF NEGOTIATION and I ask him if he wants a cup of tea, which it turns out he does and then I *utterly casually* say, "Can I use your computer, please?" and he is quiet for quite a long time while I fidget on one leg and then he finally says, "OK, but don't step on any of my stuff."

This is not an easy thing to ask me not to do because Kurt's stuff is everywhere.

That's how he likes it, mainly on the floor.

I have to push quite hard on the door because there is something pushing back on the other side.

It turns out to be lots of T-shirts. Luckily it isn't too hard to find the computer because I know where it is meant to be.

I check my e-mails and I am exceptionordinarily pleased to see there is one from Bottyp.Moody@fidgoty.uo

It says:

Hello CB,

Have you heard about the new Ruby Redfort movie, **Run, Ruby, Run**??? It is going to be out this Christmas! I am so excited that you are in it—acting.

Too bad we can't go and see it together—
it would be really fun.
Sorry I haven't written before but our
Internet thingy has only just been set up.
I am in my new house upstairs in my new
bedroom.
I am exceptionordinarily bored and in
a minute we have to go to a barbecue where
Cecil and Mol hope I will meet some new
friends.
What are you doing?
Whatever it is I wish I was doing it too.
Love, your friend, Betty P. Moody
P.S. Bored beyond belief!!!

I look at what she has said about **Run, Ruby, Run**
and I want to tell her about the premiere tickets and
how I had this surprise worked out but at the same
time I don't—it just seems too sad to write—
so instead I say:

Dear Betty,
School is the same but not the same.

There is a new girl called Clem Hansson.
Mrs. Wilberton has put her next to me in
your seat.
Everyone is talking about her like mad but
it's just because she is from abroad.
I find her very unfriendly and also dreary.
I wish you would come back.
Love, CB
P.S. I still haven't moved into my new room.
P.P.S. Yes I heard about the Ruby movie.

I go up to the attic room and lift up the wobbly
floorboard so I can put my books back in the gap.
I look at the **Run, Ruby, Run** tickets and the
envelope with the invisible fly and I feel happy and
sad at the same time.

Sad because Betty isn't here and happy because
even though Betty is not here, she does wish she was.

Sometimes people can't see past a Pretty Face

18

School is a bit chilly because Mr. Skippard, the janitor, has decided to paint the coatroom and has opened all the doors to let the fumes out. He says he has to do it because someone has green-felt-tip-markered some rude words all over the walls and no one knows who did it but as usual Karl Wrenbury has to go see Mr. Pickering, because "He is always a suspect."

That's what Mrs. Marse, the school secretary, says. I know it wasn't Karl because most of the rude words were about Benji Murtle and Karl would never write rude words about Benji Murtle.

Mr. Skippard says, "It must have happened last night during gymnastics."

When we come out of assembly, I happen to be

standing next to Clem when this big green marker falls out of her coat pocket.

Neither of us says anything.

She looks down at it as if she has never seen it before and then she looks at me and blinks.

I can't imagine why she would have a big green marker or why she would write rude words about people on the walls—especially since she doesn't really know anyone well enough to be rude about them. But she must have got under the spell of Justin Broach and now is *desperate* to impress him.

Before class there is a bag search but they don't find the pen and I don't say a word.

After school I go up to Karl and I say he should be careful of getting in trouble again, because does he remember what Mr. Pickering said and how he was on his last chance. And Karl says he's not going to get in trouble and I say well you should be careful about hanging around with Clem Hansson because I have got a bad feeling about her.

And then Karl gets all annoyed with me and says, "You don't know what you're talking about. Clem is really nice." And I say, "All I'm saying is watch out."

And Karl says, "You have been reading too much Ruby Redfort." And then he does this impression of me walking along reading my Ruby Redfort books and it is quite good and then I do one of him messing around with Toby Hawkling—and he tries not to laugh but he can't not because it is *utterly* funny.

On my way home, I see Clem Hansson, she is walking along with Justin Broach and the boy with the odd haircut. I watch them for a bit and I see Justin Broach go to snatch her hat but she grabs onto it and then they all start running after each other. I decide to walk up the hill a bit because I don't want to have to say hello or not say hello.

Mr. Enkledorf is on the hill—he likes to go up there to watch the dogs. There are always lots of them running around and barking and doing what dogs do. Mr. Enkledorf misses having a dog, but he is not allowed one at the old persons' center—so for him watching dogs is the next best thing.

In the distance I can see Karl and his brother Alf. They are kicking a soccer ball around.

It is getting a bit wintry and I like that—not cold completely but leaves beginning to go slightly curly and dead at the edges and I like that even though it is a bit sad.

I am not sure why it is a bit sad but it somehow is and I quite like the feeling in a strange way.

On the corner I bump into Kira. She is standing chatting with Marcie's friend Stan.

When Kira sees me, she shouts,

"Hey there, kiddo. How's it going?"

I say, "How's what going?"

And Kira starts laughing and she says to Stan, "This kid just has me in stitches, man. *I just love this kid.*"

And Stan laughs too and that's the first time I have seen Stan laugh in a friendly sort of way.

And then Stan says, "Is your brother still seeing that drip Saffron?"

And I say, "I thought she was called Amber," and I notice that Kira's face goes all tight, just for a second, and then she laughs and says, "Yep, he sure knows how to pick 'em, right?"

Out of the corner of my eye I see Justin Broach coming across the road from the park but when he catches sight of Stan, he changes his mind and walks the other way.

And I am surprised when Stan says, "There goes that loser cousin of mine."

Kira gives me a piece of chewing gum and I walk off home and then Stan calls out,

"Hey, Clarice Bean,
tell Marce I'll be
over later—OK?"

When I get in, I tell Marcie Stan's message and I say, "Hey, I never knew Justin Broach was Stan's cousin."

And Marcie says, "How come you were talking to Stan?" You see I normally never get to talk to her friends.

And I say, "Because I bumped into Kira outside the shop and we were chatting about things."

When I say this, Kurt looks up from his magazine, as if he is waiting for me to say something else.

Marcie looks at him and says, "Is that drip Jasmine coming over later?"

And Kurt says, "She's called Amber, and yeah, she is."

And Marcie says, "Oh boy, I'm getting out of here." Then she looks at me and does this eye signal that I think means, *And so should you.*

When I go into the kitchen, I see there is a note on the table next to some cookies, and the cookies look different from normal cookies I am used to seeing, and the note just says one word: ciastka. I decide they must be Polish cookies from Jacek, which means Dad must have sorted things out with Town Hall. I think ciastka is a useful word to remember if I am ever in Poland. They look very interesting and I think I might nibble one with a drink. I take one bite and since there are no plates I put it in my coat pocket so it doesn't get dusty while I am looking for the milk, which—when I find it—is not in the fridge and is now at body temperature and cannot safely be smelled without making me feel queasy.

Since Kurt is distracted with a magazine, I go off to see if Betty has e-mailed me back.

And she has.

Hi CB,
Yesterday was not so bad as I thought it
would be.
All the people were very nice—sort of—
except this one girl called Quincy who thinks
she is so great.
She has got this really loud voice and
she just goes on and on about herself
all the time.
Why is that girl Clem Hansson so bad?
Is she like that girl Sadie Blanche in
Run, Ruby, Run, the one that tries to get in
with Clancy Crew?
Anyway, what's going on back home?
Anything exciting happened since I left?
Love, Betty P. Moody xxxx

If you don't know it, Sadie Blanche arrives at
Ruby's school and she is really tall and pretty and
perfect-looking and Clancy Crew goes into a weird
T R A N C E   about her and keeps asking her on a

date to the movies. Although actually Sadie Blanche is in with Vapona Bugwart and Ruby discovers that she is a *utter phony* and also a meanie.

Betty Moody's e-mail makes me even more worried about Karl than before. Because you see it is true—Clem Hansson is very like Sadie Blanche, and Clancy Crew got in really big trouble because of her and if it wasn't for Ruby Redfort, who knows what would have happened?

Ruby said, "Clance, just because a person has a cute face it don't mean they are made of candy."

I write:

Hi Betty,
Yes, you are right—Clem Hansson is exactly like Sadie Blanche and she is trying to get in with everybody especially Karl Wrenbury and she is most likely going to get him in big trouble because she is a friend of Justin Broach and Justin Broach is as you know Karl's archenemy. And Justin Broach and Clem Hansson wrote mean things about Benji

Murtle and Karl almost got the blame for it. Anyway, I am worried it could mean curtains for Karl at this school.

Czarina has stopped teaching drama due to an expected baby and more of our house has fallen down.

That girl Quincy sounds exceptionordinarily annoying but at least she is just a show-off which is better than a meanie.

Talk to you tomorrow or soon.

Love, CB

I get out my Worst Worry Notebook and write WORRY no. 13: Karl Wrenbury getting in big trouble. This is a WORST WORRY but it is not a WORST WORRY I DIDN'T EVEN THINK TO WORRY ABOUT because I worried about it all last spring and I was the only one who could save him but this time I don't think I can.

There's no such thing as Too Much Information — or is there?

19

A few days later, I have a really bad day at school. I am very tired due to the not sleeping and Mrs. Wilberton makes us do this spelling test with *utterly* no warning. Even though I do actually know some of the words, my brain is too exhausted to remember and I do really badly. Mrs. Wilberton goes on about how *amazing* it is that Clem Hansson, who is *foreign from Sweden,* manages to be a better speller than me. She says, "You should try to go to bed a bit earlier, young lady, rather than sitting around watching television until all hours."

I say, "But we haven't even got a television anymore."

And she says, "Give me a break."

I can see Grace Grapello thinking this is very funny.

After school I am walking down Sesame Park
Road. It is a bit blowy and I can feel this brown
paper bag following me—
it won't leave me alone.

I even cross over to the other side of the street
and it is still there, right behind me.

It's as if Robert Granger has turned himself into
a piece of litter.

What I end up doing is jumping on it,
to squash it.

Just as I am doing this, Kira walks out of Eggplant.
She is with this boy.

He has dark hair—a bit straggly—and a large coat.

I notice that he is very attractive. Kira is laughing
her head off, but Kira laughs her head off a lot.

So who knows if he is funny?

She says, "Hey, Josh, this is Kurt's kid sister,
Clarice Bean. She's funny, man."

Josh says, "Hey there."

And I can't think of anything to say so I say,
"Hey there," back.

Kira says, "So what are you up to?"

And I say, "Just trying to squash this paper bag."

And she says, "See what I mean? She cracks me up, man." The boy called Josh nods.

I am not sure what she means, so I don't nod.

Kira says, "Hey, see you in the shop sometime, huh?"

I say, "Uh-*huh*."

Then they walk off. When they get to the corner, the boy says something and Kira takes the chewing gum out of her mouth and they kiss each other for quite a long time without taking a breath.

When they stop, Kira puts the gum back in.

I am not just standing there watching or anything— I am slightly seeing by accident. I am actually looking in the Eggplant window but I can't help noticing them at the same time. It's in the reflection. And in any case it is a Ruby technique that she would use if she was tailing someone, and it is important to practice these skills—that's what Ruby would say.

"A good spy will brush up on his or her spy skills whenever the chance is there. Remember, a prepared spy is a spy—an unprepared spy is just another member of the public."

Anyway, of course this is very bad news because

I was hoping my brother would come to his senses and go out with Kira because I would like it if she was hanging out at our house but now it is too late.

When I walk into the shop, Kurt is pricing up lots of tins of tomatoes.

He is doing it really fast and almost bashing the cans with his pricing thingy.

Quite a lot of them have dents. He has a fierce-ish look on his face.

I look at Waldo Park and he does a sort of eye signal to me that I think means, *"I would keep out of his way if I were you. I am not even going to tell him to stop denting the cans because I don't think he will take it well."*

It's amazing what the human face can say with just one look—Ruby's got this whole section at the back of her **SPY GUIDE**. It basically shows you how to use your face to convey rather a lot of information to your spy accomplice and do things with your face that are code.

When I get in, Marcie is chatting to Stan in the kitchen. Stan is saying to Marcie, "I saw your brother earlier and he is in a really bad mood. What's gotten into him? He didn't even say hello."

And Marcie says, "Don't ask me—maybe he has just realized how boring Saffron is."

And Stan says, "Amber."

And Marcie says, "Amber, Jasmine, Chloe—why *wouldn't* he be depressed?"

And Stan says, "Nah, it can't be because of that—your brother is crazy about boring girls."

And I say, "I know why."

And they both look up.

And I say, "I know why Kurt is in a bad mood."

And they both say, "Why?"

And I say, "Because of Kira."

And Marcie says, "Why because of Kira?"

And I say, "Because of Kira and Josh. Kurt does not like Kira having an attractive boyfriend called Josh."

And Marcie and Stan look at each other and say, "*Ohhhh.*"

And then Marcie says, "How do you know?"

And I say, "Because I have been reading this book called *THE RUBY REDFORT SPY GUIDE: HOW TO KNOW THINGS WITHOUT KNOWING THINGS*, and it tells you all about body language and facial expressions."

And I tell them about how Kira was kissing outside the shop and how Kurt was bashing the cans of tomatoes and it's because he was annoyed.

And Stan says, "That explains why Kira said she was looking for a new job."

And Marcie says, "They are obviously crazy about each other."

Stan says, "Hey, can I see your book?"

And Marcie looks a bit amazed that she would ask this but when they have a look they both actually in fact find **THE RUBY REDFORT SPY GUIDE** very fascinating.

I can tell they are quite impressed that I have worked this out about Kurt but I just walk out of the room like it is all utterly obvious and go upstairs to check if there is an e-mail from Betty.

And there is.

Hi CB,
That new girl sounds dreadful—she must be trying to be being friends with Justin Broach. Do you really think Karl Wrenbury is going to end up in big trouble—have you told him???

Talking of dreadfulish girls . . .
I have been asked to join the swimming club
and I am OK at swimming so I said yes, but
guess who is the captain? That girl Quincy.
What a surprise huh?
What's going on with you?
What's happened about your new room?
Are you going to be in the Christmas play?
Do we have a new teacher yet?
Love, Betty P. Moody

I look at what she has written—"Do *we* have a new
teacher yet?"

And I think maybe she is coming back—or why
would she write "Do *we* have a new teacher?"
Maybe call me Cecil and call-me-Mol have realized
that it is unfair to take Betty away. Maybe they really
are going to send her back.

I write:

Hello Betty,
We do not yet have a new teacher—
worst luck—but don't worry by the time that

Cecil and Mol decide to bring you back we
will. I am not sure about the Christmas play—
I don't really feel like acting.
And nothing much is going on with me except
my room is still not finished although it is
about to get a radiator.
It sounds like Kira is going to leave Eggplant.
Love, your friend, CB
P.S. Yes, I have told Karl to watch out, but
you know Karl—he just never listens.

I nip up to the attic to see what the Polish builders
have done. I right away notice there is a note on the
radiator, but unfortunately I also notice there is
a spider standing on the note.

I am not a baby about spiders, but I do not like the
ones who seem to have fur. I have a quick look in
THE SURVIVAL HANDBOOK to see what I should
do and discover that Ruby herself doesn't have an
actual chapter on this problem because to Ruby, apart
from poisonous tarantula-type ones, spiders are merely
creatures with eight legs like any other insect—
although strictly speaking, they are not an insect.

She does however have a section called
WASTE-OF-TIME WORRIES AND FOOLISH FEARS.

Ruby says, "If you want, you can choose to spend a whole heap of time making a big deal about things that are totally pointless, but why bother when there are plenty of life and death problems to keep you awake sweating for the rest of your days?"

I decide Ruby has a point but I am still not sure how I am going to get the spider off the note. Luckily when I call downstairs for help, Jacek is still there—he is having a cup of tea with Grandad. He manages to remove the spider in 2 seconds—he doesn't seem at all frightened and then he hands me the note. It just has one word on it: kaloryfer, so I am guessing it means either "spider" or "radiator" in Polish.

I realize that maybe a useful phrase to learn would be, "There is a spider on my radiator." Or maybe even better, "There is a spider in my room." Because you see spiders are not always on the radiator.

Jacek says in Polish this is, "W moim pokoju jest pająk." After he has gone, I think to myself that if I learn the phrase "There is a spider in my room" in all sorts of different languages, then wherever I am, I will always be able to ask for help.

I start by calling Uncle Ted's girlfriend, Stina, and asking her what "There is a spider in my room" is in Swedish.

She is really nice and says it is, "**Det är en spindel i mitt rum**." She says she will send me an actual Swedish dictionary if I want—in case there is anything else I want to look up. And I am pleased because you can never have too much information— that's what Ruby Redfort says.

What to do when you are Surrounded by a Pack of Wolves

The next day I am woken by another very unusual sound. It is two people being very annoyed at each other, which is not particularly strange in our house—but the thing which is strange is that it is Mom and Dad being annoyed at each other.

And I am not saying that they are never the sort of people who tell each other off or that they don't get annoyed with each other, ever   just that they never get annoyed with each other like this. This is the kind of argument that Kurt and Marcie would have *or* me and Marcie *or* Minal and Marcie *or* me and Minal.

Not Mom and Dad.

I go into the kitchen and try to find something to eat that isn't toast.

This problem is solved by the fact the bread is covered in a thick layer of ceilingish dust—and it is not edible—so there is no toast.

Dad says to Mom, "Why did you leave the bread out? Are you *crazy?*"

Mom says, "Well, if you would actually come home from work once in a while, maybe you could discover where the bread bin has gotten to—because I certainly can't."

Dad says, "Well, perhaps you have forgotten but someone's got to earn some money to pay to get the ceiling mended."

And Mom says, "I don't know why you are bothering—I just love being able to see down into the kitchen when I am using the toilet."

Dad says, "Well, I am sorry to spoil such an attractive feature but it is being fixed. I told you I would sort it out and I have."

And Mom looks up at the ceiling and says, "Well, perhaps I am *blind as a bat* but it doesn't look like anyone has mended it to me—oh, is that Minal taking a bath or Marcie?"

I can feel all my hairs going up on my arms

because although it might sound funny if they are not people you know—i.e., not your mom and dad—it isn't funny if you do know them, because what I know and you don't know unless you do know them is that they never fight like this—they always make their arguments funny and Dad always kisses her, even if he is quite sure he is right and she is wrong. He always kisses her, and he never goes to work without kissing her.

But this time he does.

And things are not good in my family and everyone is beginning to turn on everyone else.

I am walking to school thinking about Ruby's chapter on WHAT TO DO IF YOU ARE LOST IN A FOREST, SURROUNDED BY AN ANGRY PACK OF WOLVES.

This is a tricky one because you are both lost and surrounded by wolves, but the clue is, you are in a forest—and what forests are made of is trees. And if you know what wolves are—actually dogs—you will get the idea because dogs cannot climb trees.

They often think they can.

But they can't.

So you must *absolutely* climb a tree, speedily.

This will also help you find out where you are because you will have a good view.

You must wait up there until dawn because that is when wolves go to bed.

If you should be lucky enough to have some matches, you can light a fire, because wolves also do not like fire.

The problem is, it can be very awkward to get a campfire going while you are surrounded by wolves and they will probably have eaten you by the time you have collected enough twigs to get it started.

When I get to school, I tell Karl Wrenbury about this emergency solution.

He says he wouldn't do either of these two things. He would simply get down on all fours and start howling. He said he would just in fact trick the wolves into thinking he was a wolf himself.

And what's more, he would trick them into thinking he was their pack leader and they would all trust him and they would show him the way out of the forest and then while they were all sleeping he would manage to escape.

Karl Wrenbury says, "Wolves are easy; it's bears that are the problem."

Karl is right because I looked bears up on the Internet and I have discovered that they are fast runners. Also excellent sniffers. *They can even smell if you have half a crumbled cheese cracker in your pocket—* they will know, even if *you* don't know it yourself and it has actually been there since you went on a school trip to the science museum.

So rule one is check your pockets for old bits of food because even a slightly sucked cough drop will attract a bear.

The other thing about bears is that not only can they run, but they can climb trees too and also swim and dig.

What they cannot do is fly.

But then neither can I—so I don't really see how this helps.

Ruby says,
"What to do if you meet a bear—
                    wish you hadn't."

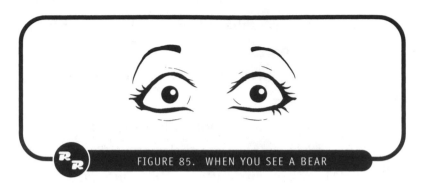

FIGURE 85. WHEN YOU SEE A BEAR

At the end of school, I notice Karl hanging around at the school gates. He is smiling at Clem Hansson like mad, but she is busy chatting with Grace Grapello and Cindy Fisher and doesn't seem to notice.

I am cheered up when I get home because there is an e-mail from Betty.

Hi there CB,
School is still super dull except we get
to do these quite cool things afterward—
like surfing.
I am trying to get Mol and Cecil to buy me
a board—otherwise I will just have to stand

around like a twit in a bathing suit.

That girl Quincy said I could borrow her
brother's board but I am not sure I want to
get in with her.

I've got to rush because Mol and Cecil are
taking me out for Chinese—did you know this
is one of the best towns if you like to eat
Chinese food and I am crazy about Chinese
food.

Catch you later, Be

P.S. What a drag about Karl.

Be? Why is she signing her name *Be*?

And why would she even *think* of getting in with
that girl Quincy?

And what does she mean "what a drag about
Karl"—it is more than a drag—it is very serious.

I flick through **THE RUBY REDFORT
SURVIVAL HANDBOOK** to see if she has got any
good advice about what to do when people go a bit
weird—but she doesn't.

I decide Betty must be a bit off-color due to
delayed jet lag or perhaps a strange virus and I am

just about to write back when the telephone starts
ringing.

It's Dad. He just says, "I am stuck here for at least
two more hours—tell your mother and save me
some toast. On second thought, scrap the toast.
I'll get something to eat on my way home."

He sounds very cranky about it.

I go back to the computer and write:

Hi Betty,
I wish we could go out and eat Chinese food—
all we get to do these days is eat toast.
I have decided not to be in the school play.

Before I can write any more, I get interrupted
by a very loud banging on the door. It goes on for
some time and I just sit there wondering who it is,
and finally I go downstairs and call through the
mail slot.

I say, "Who is it, please?"

And the annoyed voice says, "*Me,* your mother."

And I say, "But why aren't you using your keys?"

And she says, "Because Mr. Larsson managed to

'accidentally' tip my handbag upside down and they fell down a heating vent. Now could you please just

open the blimming door?"

When I let her in, the first thing she says is, "Where is your wretched father?"

I say he called and said he would be back late. Then I make a run for it.

I finish writing my e-mail quickly in case Kurt comes back.

```
Everyone here is in an
exceptionordinarily bad mood.
Love, CB
```

Sometimes People gotta Say what they gotta Say

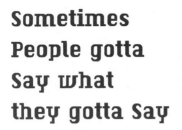

When I go back downstairs, Mom is in Grandad's room telling him about her bad day.

Grandad is nodding and sensibly not saying anything except for the odd tutting sound—which is the right thing to do. Grandad is obviously an expert at calming people down.

Ruby Redfort herself would say, "HOW TO DEAL WITH AN ANGRY INDIVIDUAL: Let 'em talk—just make soothing noises and calming gestures. WARNING: DO NOT TRY TO ARGUE WITH THEM. EVEN REASONING CAN BE RISKY IF THEY ARE VERY MAD."

Mr. Larsson has been acting up again and driving everyone around the bend.

Mom says, "He got very irritable because he had run out of pickled herring. He likes to have them on a slice of rye bread with beets."

Mom says, "I have enough of my own worries to be dealing with without having to run around trying to locate herring.

"Plus while he was busy tipping my handbag upside down, he also managed to get his walker stuck in the heating vent—how he managed it I don't know but it really was the last straw."

Grandad nods and tuts and says, "*Mmm,* a very tricky man."

Mom says, "You can say that again."

And Grandad says, "*Mmm,* a very tricky man," and he pats Mom on the arm and she sort of looks a bit better and pops some toast in the toaster.

Ruby says,

"Sometimes people gotta say what they gotta say—then they feel fine."

In the morning I get up and nip into the bathroom to brush my teeth before Marcie or Kurt can get in there. Kurt has been much more interested in washing since he started going out with Amber and Chloe and Jasmine and What's-her-name. Mom says it happened when he realized girls like boys to smell clean even if they *look dirty*.

We all do prefer him being clean but we only have one bathroom so it makes it very hard to get a turn. I have gotten quite good at avoiding the hole in the floor and it is useful because I can keep an eye on the kitchen at the same time.

What I see is Mom putting her coat on—she has to leave early because it is her day to go and work at the old persons' center.

And she is asking Dad if he has called Town Hall to arrange for the rubble to be taken away like he promised to do.

And Dad is saying no that he didn't have time and forgot and didn't get around to it and that he is sorry and he meant to and he is rambling on like a drowning man.

And then he says, "T, let's go out tonight, you and me, no more toast."

And Mom says, "You know what, I just can't be bothered."

And   walks   off.

This gives me a chill because Mom absolutely never says, "I can't be bothered"; in fact she never lets any of us say it either. She says it is *the most depressing phrase in the English language.* She says people who say that they can't be bothered have given up and one should only give up when there really is nothing else to be done.

And now I am beginning to think that THE WORST WORRY I DIDN'T EVEN THINK TO WORRY ABOUT is much worse than the moving WORST WORRY. Because it seems that THE WORST WORRY I DIDN'T EVEN THINK TO WORRY ABOUT is my mom and dad getting divorced, and it's funny in a strange kind of way, that all the time when I thought it was me moving it was actually Betty.

And all the time I thought it was Betty's mom and dad getting divorced it was in fact mine.

And maybe it will be like how it is for Karl Wrenbury, and my dad will move away somewhere and not tell us where he has gone—except it will more likely be my mom because

she is sick of all of us
    and
      fed up to the ears with
        everything.
    I get out my notebook to write down **WORST WORRY:** Mom and Dad getting divorced but then I stop because I don't want it written down in writing because it is too worse a worry to look at. I go to bed but I can sleep hardly a wink.

What to do when there are No Passing Planes

Nearly all night long I can hardly sleep and when I arrive at school I am late. There is nobody around except for four people and I am *utterly* amazed to see Karl gripping onto Justin Broach's arm, which is around Karl's neck. I am not sure what is happening at first—it is difficult to see. They almost look like they are having fun, kind of like when Minal and Kurt do wrestling and Kurt always makes out that Minal is winning, because he is so small.

But when they twist around, I see that Justin Broach is *not* letting Karl win and they are *not* having fun— at least Karl isn't, and blood is trickling out of Karl's nose and onto his sweater. His mom won't be pleased because I happen to know it is new for school.

Benji Murtle—the boy who sits at the back of our

class not talking—is picking up lots of colored pens off the pavement—they are spread out like a rainbow. Clem is running indoors, and she has left her bag on the ground. I expect she's going to tell Mr. Skippard even though it is most likely her fault that they are fighting in the first place.

I knew she would get Karl into trouble and now I can cross **WORRY no. 13** off my list because it is not a worry anymore; it is *true*. And now my new worry is **WORRY no. 14: Karl Wrenbury getting asked to leave our school.**

Mr. Skippard comes out and takes Justin Broach and Karl by the arms and marches them into school. Karl is late for class because he has to go and get some cotton stuck up his nose. When I see Justin Broach at recess, he doesn't look like he has been in a fight at all—even his hair is still all neat.

When I get home, I go to the fridge but it isn't there. It takes me a while to find it. It's in Grandad's room, and he doesn't seem too bothered—he says it's handy for the cheese.

I decide I might as well stay in his room until

suppertime because everywhere else is not where it should be and I am more likely to get fed if I am in the room with the fridge.

Later when Kurt has gone out, I sneak into his room to check for e-mails from Betty but there isn't one. And I am just about to write her one when I hear Kurt slam the front door—so I nip out super-fast.

That weekend goes very slowly—there is nowhere to be on my own and the weather is more and more dreary by the minute. Mom seems to be at the old persons' center most of the time and Dad isn't his normal self. And when Minal accidentally shakes tomato ketchup all over Dad's coat, Dad is not very nice about it. Minal says, "Sorry." And Dad says, "Sometimes sorry just isn't good enough."

He ends up spending most of the weekend in his work room and he is not doing very much communicating. He seems to have turned into Kurt. I decide that I will tell Granny about his strange behavior—she is his mother and she might know what to do.

Luckily for me, she said she would call on Monday, which is tomorrow. Meanwhile I make an extra note in my **Worst Worries Notebook**—under

WORRY no. 15: people behaving not like themselves.

On Monday I rush out of school so I won't be late for Granny's phone call. I am in such a hurry to get out of there that I forget my bag and when I nip back to the pegs I see Clem Hansson hanging around with Justin Broach. She is giving him some of her sweets.

When I get home, I make a drink and sit with a plate of cookies next to the telephone. After a while I lose track of how long I have been sitting there because it just keeps not ringing and my mind starts to w a n d e r o f f.

Minal is hopping up and down stairs and I say, "Can you please go and hop off somewhere else because I am waiting for a *very important* call."

And he says, "No, you're not."

And I say, "Yes, I am actually, twit."

And he says, "Uh-uh."

And I say, "What do you mean, *uh-uh*?"

And he says, "The phone has been unwired and it doesn't work because the builders broke it."

I say, "Thanks for telling me."

And he says, "I just did."

And I say, "Yes, you *just* did—

when you could have told me

47 at least minutes ago,

you worm."

Then I throw a moldyish tomato

at him and it splats on the wall

and he chucks a glass of water,

which misses by a mile,

and I fling an already used

tea bag and he knocks over

a whole thing of juice

and I am about to start throwing a bowl of clementines when we hear the key in the front door.

And we both freeze because it will be Mom and I say, "We have to tidy it up before she sees because she will be mad and possibly leave." And Minal says,

"Why? *Why* will she leave?" And I say, "Because of her and Dad probably getting a divorce." And Minal starts going all whimpery and I say, "You mustn't say. Whatever you do, *keep it zipped*." And Minal nods but he is not someone to tell a secret to and I just know he will blab.

I have broken one of the most important Ruby Redfort rules: "NEVER TELL A SECRET TO A BLABBERMOUTH." And I have just made another worry for myself, **WORRY no. 16: telling a little big-mouth something no one is supposed to know.**

And just at that moment Jacek walks in. He looks at me and then he looks at Minal and then he looks at the walls. He goes out and closes the door behind him and I can hear him say to Mom, "Don't go into the kitchen for now—we are just having a cleanup." And then Jacek sticks his head around the door and says, "Posprzątaj szybko."*

Minal and me madly start running about cleaning up. And I realize something—there is no one I can talk to about my worst worry—THE WORRY I DIDN'T EVEN THINK TO WORRY ABOUT

* Polish for "*Hurry—clean up.*"

because of course I can't tell Granny because she is related and will get upset and I would normally maybe talk to Mom but it is *her* who is the worry and I wish I could call Betty but there is no phone.

I am thinking about this Ruby Redfort survival emergency called, HOW TO MAKE CONTACT WHEN YOU HAVE NO TRANSMITTER.

Ruby says, "You should make a big fire or write a big S.O.S. sign in branches so that a passing plane can read it."

But what I want to know is, what do you do when there are no passing planes?

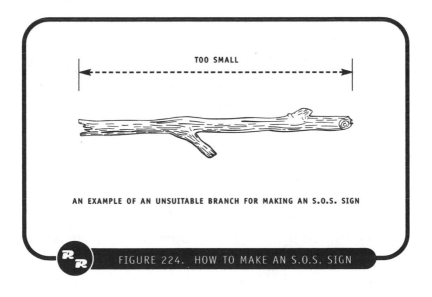

TOO SMALL

AN EXAMPLE OF AN UNSUITABLE BRANCH FOR MAKING AN S.O.S. SIGN

FIGURE 224. HOW TO MAKE AN S.O.S. SIGN

Secret Signals are only Signals if someone knows What your Signal is

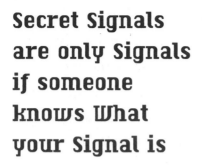

A week or so later, I am just walking into school and I see Clem Hansson being dropped off by her mother. Not in a car—they are both on bikes. Mrs. Hansson is very pretty and looks a bit like Clem but with brown hair. I notice she doesn't just leave but goes over to meet Clem's friends. She doesn't see me because she is too busy talking to Grace Grapello and Karl and people, and I just go off to wait by the doors. I just sort of perch on the steps and read my **RUBY REDFORT SURVIVAL HANDBOOK**.

When I look up, I see Clem Hansson dragging across the playground—she is coming toward me but isn't looking at me and I am surprised when she stops and sort of rummages around in her pocket. She hands me an envelope and says, "It's an invitation—it's for my party." And she is sort of looking around as if she doesn't want anyone to see that she is talking to me. And I wonder why she is inviting *me* to something— and then I think probably because her mother made her because she is asking everybody else and mothers like fairness and they make you do things like this. She just stands there waiting for something— I am not sure what.

And I slightly shuffle about in my bag as if I am looking for something and she says, "It's on Saturday the 27th."

And I say, "Oh."

And she says, "Do you think you can come? It's at 4 o'clock."

And I wonder why she has bothered to make the invitation if she is just going to tell me everything without letting me read it all first.

I say,
"Well, I will have to ask—I am not sure if I can. It's over fall break—I will most likely be quite busy."

And she just says, "OK." She is looking at my book and also staring weirdly at my coat and I almost think she's going to ask me something but then she sees Justin Broach and walks off.

I can tell she is quite relieved and the only reason she would want *me* there is to get more presents. Everybody else will be going anyway. She is bound to have invited everyone in the whole school; probably even Justin Broach is going.

When I get home, I don't bother to tell my mom about Clem Hansson's party—she would only want me to go. She likes people to do the friendly thing. I don't want her to find the invitation. I haven't even bothered to open it.

I pull out my sock drawer and stuff it into a pair of stripy tights.

Fall break is usually a time I look forward to because there is normally too much to do and Betty and me find there is not enough hours in the day. But this vacation is no fun at all. Karl is busy for the first part because he has got some cousins visiting and he said I could still come over but I don't really feel like it. And Noah has gone away and also my friend Suzie Woo has gone away and people just aren't around and I haven't planned anything.

Mainly I just go for walks and read my Ruby books and hang around not doing much.

The weather is nice, though—it is all crispy and cold with no wind mainly, and when I go up to the top of the hill I can see for a long, long way.

And sometimes I think that things far away look much nicer than things up close.

On Wednesday, in the distance I can see Karl and his brother Alf. They are kicking a soccer ball around with their cousins. And I also see my friend Lucy Mackay shopping with her mom. She waves at me and I wave back but I don't go over to talk to her— I just keep walking.

I stop off at Eggplant to have a smoothie. I don't feel like going home yet because it will be too noisy. I am sitting at the counter with my Ruby book and Kira says,

"Hey, kiddo, what you reading?"

And I say,

"HOW TO SECRETLY SIGNAL TO AN ACCOMPLICE. It's from **THE RUBY REDFORT SPY GUIDE**."

And she says, "Cool, I always wanted to be a spy when I was a kid—what's it say?"

And I say, "Well, I am reading this bit about secret signals for when you are in distress and need the help of your spy accomplice and you have to do this thing called a hand blink—look," and I show her the illustration. "Ruby says, 'It is vital your spy accomplice knows your distress signal; otherwise a grimace and a hand blink could be mistaken for a smile and a wave.'"

She says, "Hey, far out."

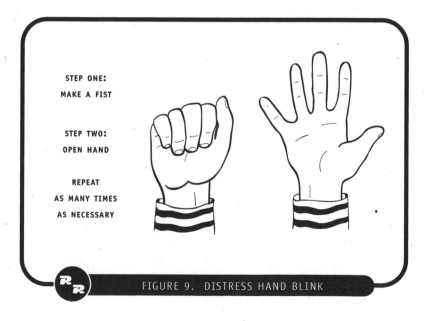

STEP ONE:
MAKE A FIST

STEP TWO:
OPEN HAND

REPEAT
AS MANY TIMES
AS NECESSARY

FIGURE 9. DISTRESS HAND BLINK

"And there is this other one you can do with just your eyes where you make them look down and then look right up—it means 'Get-me-outta-here-fast.'"

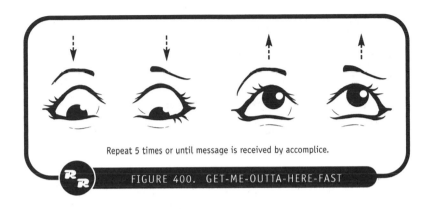

Repeat 5 times or until message is received by accomplice.

FIGURE 400. GET-ME-OUTTA-HERE-FAST

Kira is really interested. I can tell because she is really leaning over my book and she says, "This Ruby kid is a blast."

Ruby has a bit that tries to teach you how to do a loud whistle. It involves sticking your fingers in your mouth—I say to Kira that I have never been able to do this and she says, "*Really?* It's easy; you just gotta get your tongue in the right place." She does this really extremely loud whistle and I wish I could do it because as Ruby says,

"If you can't hear that, you can't hear anything."

On my way home, I walk back through the park and over the hill. I can see Mr. Enkledorf far off. He is wending his way over to the old persons' center. Behind him are Justin Broach and the boy with the odd haircut—they are impersonating his walk, which is mean because he is an extremely old person with a dodgy back and I wonder how they would walk if they were nearly 100ish or more.

When I get home, I realize that I am feeling quite utterly bad.

I think about all the things that have happened and about all THE WORST WORRIES THAT I DIDN'T EVEN THINK TO WORRY ABOUT that are on their way.

And I start to feel sick inside and I know things will not get better; they will just keep getting worse and there is only one person I feel like talking to and maybe she is the only one who can help.

Sometimes you say what you Gotta say and just Feel Worse

The house is very quiet and so I tiptoe up to Kurt's room—luckily, he's not in—and I sit in front of the computer.

I decide I must tell Betty how I am feeling—she will know what to do.

I write:

Hello Betty,

Things are getting much worse.

I am not sleeping at all and now I am doing really badly in school because my brain is in slow motion.

I am worried about Karl—he has been fighting with Justin Broach and he is only doing it because he's jealous that Clem

Hansson is friends with him. She is going to
get him in really big trouble—I know it. And if
he gets in any more big trouble, you know
what will happen, he will be asked to leave
the school.
And Kira has started going out with Josh
and I wish she would go out with Kurt and
everyone is arguing and not getting along.
And my mom and dad are going to be getting
a divorce and my mom will probably move out.
The only thing I have to do over break is go
to Clem Hansson's party and why would I
want to do that?
Love, CB

I read my e-mail back to myself and it makes me
feel very sad to see what I have written because
somehow it makes it more true.

And I have my mouse on the **send** button and
I am just about to click when there is this scream—
it's Mom.

I run downstairs and what I see is Fuzzy all
covered in paint, running madly around the kitchen.

Marcie manages to grab him and gets paint all over her skirt—which as you can imagine she is not pleased about. Mom is shouting at Minal, and Minal is squealing, "*It wasn't me.*"

And Mom says, "I told you not to let Fuzzy in here and now look what's happened!"

And Minal says, "He just wriggled past me."

And Mom says, "Well, you had better get cleaning because I am going to have to spend my afternoon at the vet's." She is very angry.

Then she says, "Minal, you're a maggot!" Which if you know my mother, you know she would never say because she is the one always telling me off for calling Minal a maggot.

I go with Mom to the vet's. It takes a while to get the paint off and the vet has to clip Fuzzy's fur so that there is no toxicness that can poison him. He has to wear one of those big collar things too. When I look at Fuzzy, I am devastated because I realize there is no chance now of me entering him in the pet show, because he cannot be groomed and he is unrecognizable as a cat.

When we get back, I remember that I didn't get to actually send my e-mail to Betty and I race up to Kurt's room. What I notice is that there is in fact a message from Betty herself.

It says:

Hey there Clarice,
I am dying to tell you—as well as joining the swim team, I am also going to join the young people's theater company.
Quincy said it's super great and I will love it especially because I have already done drama workshop.
Anyway there are lots of nice people in it and they have a proper little theater and everything where you put on shows. It's really professional.
I wonder what you are doing now.
Is your room finished?
Hope you are having fun and everything is super great with you!!
X Be

I just stare at her e-mail because it gives me a strange
feeling. She doesn't really seem like Betty Moody.
And I look at the e-mail I have written to her and
I read it back to myself and then I click the **delete**
button and watch all the words disappear backward
so that the only words left are, **Hello Betty.**
Then I write:

**Things are really SUPER GREAT here and
I am having lots of fun.
My room is really nice and I have had lots
of friends over and they all are utterly
impressed and love it.
It's a shame you can't see it.
Love, Clarice Bean
P.S. I have given up acting because I am
too busy to fit it in and have too much
else to do that I find more interesting.**

Although it makes me feel better to write it,
when I click **send**, I realize I feel worse.

How to make yourself Invisible

On Saturday afternoon I have to nip out super-fast to get Mom some eggs from the shop. Grandad finds it very difficult to manage a day without an egg of some sort, usually boiled.

Eggplant is closed and there is a little notice on the door that says,

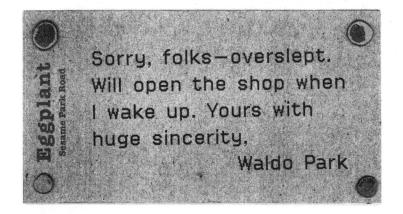

Eggplant
Sesame Park Road

Sorry, folks—overslept. Will open the shop when I wake up. Yours with huge sincerity,

Waldo Park

And of course I am puzzled as to how he can write a note if he is still asleep—or if he wrote it before he went to bed, then *how did he know* he was going to oversleep?

So I scoot over to Foxes. I am puzzling out where they might keep the organic eggs—if they have organic eggs, that is—and through the shelves I spy Karl Wrenbury. He is looking at the boxes of joke things like flies and eyeballs and those bracelets that tell you what mood you are in and things like that.

Then he starts shuffling through the card rack. He is holding up two cards, one with a painting of a rainbow on it that says, *"May All Your Birthday Wishes Come True"* and the other with a photograph of several rabbits and inside it says, *"I am hopping you will have a happy birthday."*

I can tell he isn't sure which one to get—he keeps putting one down and then picking it up again. In the end he chooses the rabbits. He is obviously buying a birthday card for Clem Hansson and today must be her party—I had *utterly* forgotten. At the

last minute he buys one of those fortune fish—
those cellophane ones you put on your hand and they
tell you what you are meant to be like.

But it only gives you about six choices of person
and not everyone can be just one out of six things.
I stay behind the cans of baked beans and chickpeas
until he has left the shop.

When I come out, I almost bump into Justin
Broach—luckily for me, he is looking the other way
and I manage to nip into the phone booth and pretend
I am making a call. It's an old Ruby technique—
I have seen her do this millions of times in the
TV show. She says, **"Faking a call is a great way
to dodge an archenemy and make yourself
invisible."**

From the phone booth I can spy on him. I watch
him cross the road—he stops and gets something
out of his bag and looks around. I think he is writing
something on the wall but I can't see what; then he
mooches off. I expect he is going to Clem's party like
everyone else.

When he has gone around the corner I nip across
the road to see what he was up to. And what I see

176

is a poster for **Run, Ruby, Run** and in green pen the words

A MoviE foR CoMplEte LoSers.

Jacek is very nice about all the paint all over the floor, much nicer than Dad was when he saw it.

He says he can fix it, but it will mean everything will be delayed because he had almost finished the kitchen.

Kurt is on his way out of the house and says, "Oh, I think your friend Betty has sent you an e-mail."

I go upstairs to look—not that I care what she has written.

It says:

Hi, Clarice
Just to warn you—Cecil and Mol are taking me to stay with Quincy's family—they have a cabin in the mountains—so I may be out of

touch for a little while. It's going to be really
good fun and they say in the summer Quincy
and me can go and visit the national park and
we might even see some bears.
I can't wait.
It was great to hear from you—
everything sounds like it is much better.
Keep me in the loop,
as Ruby Redfort would say.
Ciao for now,
X Be

What does she mean *see some bears*???

Doesn't she know what Ruby Redfort says
about bears?

I.e., "What to do if you meet a bear:
wish you hadn't."

I am not going to bother e-mailing Betty anymore
and I don't care if she is going away—she has gone
just like everybody else and has gotten in with that
Quincy girl who is probably *utterly* a show-off from
the sounds of it.

I go up to the attic to get my **RUBY REDFORT**

SURVIVAL HANDBOOK—I am thinking maybe
I should look up HOW TO DEAL WITH BEARS
but guess what? The wobbly floorboard isn't there
anymore. Well, the floorboard is there but it is not
wobbling.

I am not sure what has happened.

It is a strange mystery and very odd indeed.

And how will I ever get my book back?

And my tickets to the **Run, Ruby, Run** *premiere?*

And if only there had been a chapter on
WHAT TO DO IF YOUR SECRET HIDING PLACE
MYSTERIOUSLY DISAPPEARS.

That's the thing about Ruby—this kind of thing
never happens to her.

Is it possible to Think of Nothing?

I don't really mind going back to school for once because it has been the worst fall break I have ever had. The first thing I see is a poster up for the pet show and it just puts me in a worse mood because now even that has been ruined due to Fuzzy being bald.

I am hanging my coat up on my peg when Karl comes up to me and says, "Why are you acting so *weird*?"

And I say, "What do you mean? I don't think *I'm* the one who's acting so weird—what about *you*?"

And he says, "People are trying to be nice to you—but you don't care; you just want to be on your own not talking to anyone."

And I say, "You are only saying that because you

have got hypnotized by Clem Hansson and she likes Justin Broach and you are all jealous."

And he goes a bit red in the cheeks and says, "I am not."

And I say, "Well, why are you getting in fights with him?"

And he says, "You don't know anything."

And I say, "Well, I know you are going to get in big trouble like you did last year—and why should I help you out again? I don't know why I bothered to get in trouble for you last time!"

And he says, "I don't know why I am even bothering to talk to you."

I say, "Well, why don't you just stop bothering if it's such a big effort."

And he says, "Well, if that's what you want."

And I say, "Sure."

And he just looks at me and turns and walks away.

And I didn't mean to say that and I didn't want to say that but it's *him* that's acting weird.

Why is he making friends with Clem Hansson and Grace Grapello, and why is he bothering to have fights with Justin Broach?

And after that things seem different. Clem is not bothering to talk to me, not even *slightly,* and she is not really looking at me either. And I notice that more and more she is in the corner of the playground talking to Justin Broach. I even see her sharing her packed lunch with him—he normally just steals Benji Murtle's.

The next day at recess lots of people are gaggling around the notice board because there is a list up of who has got parts in the Christmas play.

The play is of Snow White.

I have said I don't want to be in it this year because I am not in the mood for being entertaining. Clem Hansson has got the goodish part—of Snow White—who is a bit of a drip, but it is the main role of the play and is better than *I* have ever had and *I* have been at this school for nearly almost most of my life—so it really isn't fair since she has only been here hardly any time at all.

For the next couple of nights I can't seem to sleep at all and by Thursday I am feeling a bit like I am underwater—and I am talking to less and less people—so I am really relieved when Mom calls up to me, *"Someone on the phone for you."*

It's Granny.

I tell Granny how I am being turned into almost a zombie from my situation of lack of sleep.

And that I am going a bit loopy and that maybe my brain cells are not being able to grow and that I must be getting more stupid. And I need the brain cells because I have been trying to learn Polish and I can't even remember how to say, "There is a spider in my room," which is one of the phrases I have particularly been trying to get right because it is a useful one.

Ruby says languages are particularly very important in the spy world. **"And if you ain't got 'em, how d'ya think you are gonna fool anyone?"**

Granny says, "This all sounds quite troubling. There are people who say it is good to empty your mind of all thoughts and think of nothing at all, but this seems a very complicated way of going about things to me. I always think it is easier to add more things in than take things away."

I think about math and how subtraction is harder

than addition. And how it is much harder to get rid of things than buy new ones.

Granny says, "Tibetans practice for years and years to be able to think of nothing—it is not an easy thing to do."

After I say good-bye, I go up to my *almost* room to practice thinking of nothing and right away I see how right Granny is because before I know it, I am busy thinking about what color I should paint the walls and I am thinking of green because Betty Moody always says green is a very calming color and helps you think and I am thinking about *thinking* and how I am a very good thinker already and how in fact I don't really need help with thinking— if anything I need to think less and how I wish sometimes I could think of nothing and that's when I remember the Tibetans and Granny and *how hard it is to think of nothing.*

And how right she is.

I wonder how one does keep all the bad thoughts from buzzing around in your brain—Ruby Redfort probably has this information in her **SURVIVAL HANDBOOK** but unfortunately it is trapped under the floorboards with the **Run, Ruby, Run** tickets.

And I don't even care because I don't want to go anymore. I start thinking of Betty and my surprise that I never got to surprise her with and I get out my `Worst Worries Notebook` and I write: `WORRY no. 17: bad thoughts that you can't get out of your head.`

On Friday after school, everybody is turning up with their pets. I am not staying for the pet show because I don't feel like it now that Fuzzy is not going to be in it. Clem Hansson's mother has brought Clem's rabbit in and everyone is gaggling around asking if they can hold it.

And she lets everyone have a turn, including Robert Granger, who I wouldn't trust because he has a tendency to drop things. Justin Broach goes over and even talks to Clem's mom and then Clem's mother lets him hold the rabbit too. And I think about how Justin Broach is one of those people who is really good at making grown-ups think he is nice.

And I think it is partly because of the way he looks;
he doesn't look how people expect a meanie to look
and as Ruby would say,
"People only see what they wanna see."
    And Justin Broach says, "What a sweet rabbit—
I really like rabbits."
            And if you believe that,
            you'll believe anything—

                    which it turns out
                    most people do.

The Little Things can end up as the Big Things

27

When I get to school on Monday, everybody is talking like mad and I am wondering what is going on. I forget that me and Karl aren't speaking anymore and I say, "What's going on? What's happened?"

And Karl says, "Clem's rabbit got lost at the pet show—*not that you would care.*" And he just slouches off. I am tired as a dormouse because I barely got a smidgen of sleep last night. I am desperately trying to concentrate on what Mrs. Wilberton is saying. It's hard because it is so boring. And it's hard because my eyes are closing themselves even though my brain is telling them not to.

Mrs. Wilberton starts by announcing Clem Hansson's missing Swedish rabbit and that everyone should look out for it. I am so tired with lack of sleep that I find myself nodding off a bit and have the unfortunate misfortune to find Mrs. Wilberton standing right by my desk saying, "I can see that *Clarice Bean* isn't very bothered about this, but hopefully some of you might be a little kinder. On a brighter note I would just like to say that it is Benji Murtle's birthday today."

You can tell he wishes she wouldn't bring it up because he doesn't really like to be noticed—he sits at the back of the class and mainly says nothing at all. In fact I don't even know what his voice sounds like, because he usually only says one word at a time and it's always so quiet you can hardly hear.

Mrs. Wilberton gets interrupted by Justin Broach knocking at the door—he has a note for her from Mrs. Marse. When he comes in, I notice he winks at Clem and she pretends not to see, but I do.

Mrs. Wilberton reads the note and then tells Justin Broach to wait while she rummages around trying to find whatever it was Mrs. Marse wanted in the first place.

Mrs. Wilberton carries on talking. She says,

"So Benji, what did you get for your birthday, anything nice?"

And Benji goes a bit hot in the cheeks and he says in his really quiet voice so you are lucky to even hear it, "<small>This.</small>"

It's a hat with flaps to cover your ears—it is made half from plaid and half from pretend fur.

I watch Justin Broach—he is smirking.

During recess Karl volunteers to make some posters with a photograph of the escaped rabbit.

At lunch I am running across the playground trying to nip to my favorite bench before anyone else can get there, but my shoelaces have come undone as usual—*I hate these shoes*—the laces are always coming undone. Ruby says always be careful of running with your shoelaces undone, because what happened to her one time was, she was being chased by an arch villain and then tripped and was captured and marched off to his dungeon and that was all because of an undone shoelace. Ruby says,

"It is the little mistakes you always wanna watch out for—the little things can end up as the big things."

I bend down to do them up and I am just
finishing when I hear a sort of hissing noise—it's
coming from behind the bike shed. Then I realize it
is not hissing at all, because it is in fact whispering,
but who would be whispering behind the bike shed?

I do a real Ruby Redfort technique of carrying on
tying my shoelaces even though they do not need
tying. This means if you get caught by the person
you are spying on they will never suspect, as you
have an alibi.*

There is a low voice going, "So you better have it
by Monday or else."

And then there is another quieter voice, which
says something I can't quite hear.

And I am tempted to just have a quick peek and
see who it is. I could just pretend to walk around the
corner by accident—just to see—just quickly.
But then I hear a sound that makes me change
my mind. It is the sound of laughing, not nice
laughing—it's the kind of laughing that comes from
the boy with the odd haircut. And that's when
I realize who the low whispering belongs to—
of course, it's Justin Broach.

* **Alibi** means an excuse for why you are doing something and it is proof that you are innocent.

Sometimes when you are Utterly Lost at Sea, someone will spot you

Today at school we have the lottery of which elderly old person we will be having a cup of tea with.
I wish I wasn't doing it anymore. I wish I hadn't volunteered for it, because my heart has gone out of it. But what can I do? I have to do it because Mom will be upset if I don't and now she and Dad are probably getting a divorce, and I don't want to make things actually more worse than they already are.

I also do think it is a good idea—and there are some really nice people at the old persons' center and I know quite a lot of them.

And some of them don't get that many visitors and it is a shame and so this will be nice for them.

Mrs. Wilberton does the lottery for our class. She has this big box with all the names.

Right away, Robert Granger and Arnie Singh
get Mrs. Levington—this is typical of them—
Mrs. Levington always buys nice cakes and fizzy
drinks and likes fussing about and she will be the
one making *them* tea because this is what she is like.

Noah and Suzie Woo get my favorite, Mr.
Enkledorf. But no one has got Mr. Flanders and
I like him because we share an interest in cookies
and I can always find something to talk about.

He is always saying things like, *"Now, the Fig
Newton is an interesting one. Did you know it was
invented in the 1800s, and originally they used flies
instead of figs?"* And I say something like, "Yes, I
heard that myself on the radio, and did you know
that the Oreo was discovered in South America by a
German explorer called Monsieur Von Strudel?"

I am busy thinking about Mr. Flanders and
cookies when I hear Mrs. Wilberton saying,
"Clarice Bean, would you please come up and
pick a name?"

So I go up to the box by myself; everyone else
is in a pair. I pick a little piece of folded paper and
go back to my chair. I unfold it and guess what—

I really shouldn't be surprised because of course this is how my life is going these days.

Mrs. Wilberton says, "Who is it?"

I say, "I can't really read the writing—maybe I will pick again—I think it's a blank."

Mrs. Wilberton says, "Will you stop being so ridiculous? Let me read it."

I hand the little scrunkled piece of paper to her. And Mrs. Wilberton says, "Mr. Larsson."

Nobody says anything because nobody knows about Mr. Larsson except Karl and he catches my eye and then starts fiddling with his pencil.

After all the names have been picked, I put up my hand and I say, "Mrs. Wilberton, I don't think I can have tea with Mr. Larsson."

And Mrs. Wilberton says, "Whyever not?"

And I say, "Well, the thing is you see he is a *very* difficult man and not easy to get along with and I don't think he likes people very much—especially not people who are also children."

And Mrs. Wilberton says, "So what you are saying is that Mr. Larsson *doesn't deserve to be visited—* is that right?"

And I say, "No, I am not saying he *shouldn't* be visited but just that he is the most difficult old person in the old persons' center so it is more difficult for me to visit him because I am not even in a pair."

Mrs. Wilberton is looking at me as if I am really crazy and *utterly* stupid.

She looks around the room and says, "Does anyone want to be in a pair with Clarice Bean and visit Mr. Larsson? He can't be that bad."

But of course it is too late and everyone knows I am telling the truth—they all believe me.

Karl is looking at his hands as if they are really interesting and then the bell rings and it's the end of school and that's that.

At recess I am walking across to the bench under the tree and it happens again—
the whispering voices.

But this time I can hear more of the quieter one—
I hear it saying, "But I don't have $20."

And the low voice, the Justin voice, says, "I thought

it was your birthday—I bet you got some money for that."

And then I think, it must be Benji Murtle, because it's just been his birthday and in any case Justin Broach is always picking on Benji Murtle— partly because he always has a bag of chips and Justin Broach likes chips.

When I am going out of the school gates, Justin Broach is shouting, "I like your hat, Benji."

And I am the only one who seems aware that this is not Justin Broach being nice—because of course Justin Broach does not like Benji Murtle's hat, because if he did, he would never say it; he would just take it.

I walk home very downcast.

I am just scuffing along—all the leaves have gone sort of mulchy underneath and they are sort of decayed.

Everything has just gotten even worse—and I have a new worry, WORRY no. 18: Mr. Larsson— although I think he should more likely be WORRY no. 1, since I will have to visit the most difficult, tricky, meanish old man alone, as I am just me on my own, by myself.

Behind me there is someone running and also
calling out. I am concentrating on the pavement—
I don't realize until I feel a grab on my arm that
they are calling out to me. It's Karl, and he is quite
out of breath.

I stop and look at him and he says,
"Umm. Well, I thought maybe I might, you know,
come with you because I mean I don't mind visiting
the old folk's center and I am used to tricky people."

And just like that he runs off.

And I don't even say a word.

I just stop still where I am and watch him running
to catch up with Alf.

I almost want to actually nearly slightly cry
because I am on the verge of utter relief.

It's like when Ruby Redfort got rescued by Hitch
from being marooned.
Ruby Redfort looked up—standing over her
was Hitch. There he was in his black suit
smiling. "Hey there, kid. Thought you could do
with a little company."
Ruby stared up in disbelief.

What she was thinking was, How in tarnation
did you ever find me?
But what she actually said was,
"Just when I was finally getting a little
peace and quiet around here."

The Last Thing you want to meet is a Bear

29

On Saturday afternoon I decide to go over to Karl's house. Because, you see, he said, "Why don't you come over tomorrow—if you want." And this for Karl is an actual invitation, whereas to most people it's just a suggestion which they don't expect you to do anything about.

It's all about understanding people and what they mean when they say something. Some people mean what they say and some people don't. Karl's house is in a block and all the doors are orange and it's hard to remember which is his. I by accident ring on the door next door and a very old man answers wearing a sweater with no sleeves and with his trousers rolled up strangely.

He is very pleased to see me and thinks I am

someone called Marge. He asks me how my leg is and have I brought him any digestive biscuits.

I say, "My leg is fine, thank you, but unfortunately I do not have any digestives."

He says, "Have you noticed my window boxes, Marge?"

I say, "Yes, they are lovely."

We have a bit more of a chat about all this and I am almost forgetting that he is not the one I have come to visit when luckily someone pops his head out of next door. It's Karl's little brother Alf.

He says, "Have you come to visit Karl?"

I say, "Yes, but I forgot which door was yours."

He says, "It's this orange one."

I say, "It looks just like all the other orange ones."

He says, "Except it has this big dent *here*."

I say, "Oh."

He says, "Hello, Mr. Alphonse."

Mr. Alphonse says, "Hello, Rupert. How is young Oliver?"

Alf says, "OK, thank you."

I say, "Good-bye, Mr. Alphonse."

He says, "Good-bye, Marge."

I say to Alf, "Why does he have his trousers rolled up?"

And Alf says, "Because he *likes* them rolled up."

Karl is on the sofa watching very young children's TV.

I say, "Watcha."

And he says, "Hey, CB, you came over."

I say, "How you doing, buster?"

It's just what Ruby Redfort would say to Clancy Crew.

We chat and drink some fizzies and watch a very strange program which must be for babies because *absolutely nothing* happens.

We start talking about Mr. Larsson and how he is a very scary man and Karl says the last time he was over there at the old folks' center Mr. Larsson went crazy and flung a pudding.

I say, "What do you mean?"

And Karl says, "Well, I was over at the old folks' center helping my mom take the dogs in for a visit."

If you don't know it, then what happens is every

month Karl's mom takes some pets into the old persons' center. You see, no one is allowed an animal that isn't a fish or a parakeetish bird.

And the people in charge say it is good for older people to have animals near them. They call it pet therapy—which just means helping someone feel more normal by using a pet.

Anyway, Karl says, "I am in there with two dogs, one is a sausage dog called Nipper, and the other one is Hector, not an actual particular breed, just a sort of doggish dog. Anyway, the thing about sausage dogs is that they are very short and they can get under things while nobody is noticing, and Nipper goes under Mr. Larsson's chair and he has got his bag of shopping there with some special things he has bought and what he doesn't know until he looks down is that Nipper is eating them, and so then Mr. Larsson goes bonkers."

Alf is nodding, and Karl says, "Didn't he, Alf?" And Alf says, "*Really* bonkers."

"And Mr. Larsson says, "*I was saving that ginger cake for my dessert.*" And so one of the helper lady people goes off and gets him a old folks' center dessert and gives it to him, and Mr. Larsson looks at it and he is looking and looking and then he just picks it up and *flings it at the wall*."

And I say, "What kind of dessert was it?"

And Karl says, "It was a pudding-based dessert. it might have been a trifle—I'm not sure."

Alf says, "I think it was a trifle."

And Karl says, "Yes, because there were some bits of sponge on the wall like you get at the bottom of a trifle."

I say, "*Then* what happened?"

Karl shrugs and says, "He just stormed off."

And Alf says, "He just stormed off."

I tell Karl and Alf what happened to my mom's keys and how they got lost down the heating vent because Mr. Larsson tipped Mom's handbag upside down.

And Karl says, "Crikey."

And Alf says, "Crikey."

And then I say about the herring and what happens if there aren't any.

And Karl says, "Well, he has to have herring— it's a bit like with Count Von Viscount—if he can't have eyeballs for breakfast, then he loses his powers."

And then I say, "I heard that once when they ran out of herring, he said he would eat Mr. Enkledorf's canary."

This isn't actually quite true. What he in fact said is, "What do you expect me to eat around here— that *canary*?" but it's more exciting the way I tell it.

And then Alf says, "Once when my mom went to visit with all the pets, the *turtle* went missing and my mom had to go home *without it*."

And Karl says, "Yes, that's right because actually Mr. Larsson ate it with chips."

And Alf says, "*No*, because they found it two weeks later under the sink and it was still alive and eating a sprout."

And Karl says, "No, that was a different turtle."

We are sitting there thinking about this and then Karl says, "I wonder if Mr. Larsson eats children."

And I say, "Only small ones."

And we both look at Alf and he says, "Stop it, you two."

Because you see we are all beginning to make ourselves a bit slightly worried. And I am very glad that I do not have to go and see him on my own.

And while we are talking the TV is going. And we are sitting there just goggling at the box and one program comes on after another and we don't bother to change channels—we just keep on watching.

And I am glad that we do, because on comes this program which is really interesting and almost *utterly* absorbing. It's called *Man-eaters.* And it's about wild animals who eat actual people *on purpose* and they show these reconstructions of people's lucky escapes from rhinos and lions and crocodiles and even hippopotamuses who you wouldn't think are that dangerous because they look sort of happy, but they are—*very.*

And the reason that all the people have survived is because they have managed to do the right thing. They do a reconstruction of what happened to these people in Africa who are being chased by a lion and what lions like to do is try and work out who is the easiest one to eat and so they go after the smallest, or the one with an iffy leg, and they separate them away from everybody else.

And that's what this lion did to this lady and what her husband cleverly does is get the lion's attention by riding his horse very near and shouting and the lion thinks to itself, *"Mmm, maybe I will chase him instead if he is in such a hurry to be eaten,"* and the lion stops chasing the woman and it is a brave thing for the man to do of course when you think about it, because it could be curtains for him. But luckily, the lion gets fed up and goes off to eat a zebra.

When the program is over, Alf says, "Are you really going to visit Mr. Larsson?"

And I look at Karl, hoping that he hasn't changed his mind.

And he looks at me and says, "What's the big deal? He's just a cranky old man."

But there's something about the way that he says it that makes me think he is not so sure.

When I get home, there is a package on the table, addressed to me—it's from Granny. Inside is a little white Ruby Redfort radio—it has headphones that you can plug in so you can listen in private. Her note says, *"For cluttering up your mind."*

It is one of the nicest things I have ever been given—you can carry it around with you. It has a red strap. Ruby Redfort is always listening to the radio, and she is always hearing secret messages on it just for her but of course no one else listening knows this because it is all in code.

That night I am lying in bed not sleeping, so I plug in my little headphones and switch on the radio. It's got a twisty dial and I turn it through *zillions* of different stations. I happen to find a program with a man in Bangladesh who is being interviewed about being chased by a tiger that suddenly appeared in this field where all these people were working, and somebody shouted "Tiger!" and then everyone ran and running is an absolute no-no when it comes to tigers.

Tigers are extremely speedy on their feet and you haven't got a dog's chance of being more speedy, not even if you are Olympic.

And this man knew that, but what could he do?

So he ran too but he was behind everyone else. And he had one slimmish chance of survival and that was to pretend to be dead. Imagine falling onto the floor and not twitching a muscle and just waiting for the tiger to amble over and finish you off and you just know he will be licking his chops. *But no,* the tiger was a bit put off; he didn't want to eat a dead person and he just walked off. The program is very gripping and highly interesting but even so, I am beginning to fall asleep.

I am snoozing away when suddenly I am woken up by the word bear.

A woman on the radio is saying,
"The *last thing* you want to meet is a *bear.*"

And how you can never *fight a bear* because they are *so strong* that they can pull a *actual car* apart.

And you can try playing dead—they might walk off and they might not. They are unpredictable— same as people are.

And really you see your only option is to take a chance and hope you are lucky. And even though this information is very gripping, I am finding myself nodding off and I just hear things like,

"Never have food in your pockets. . . .

The more of you the better. . . ."

And the last thing I hear

as I am drifting into sleep is,

"Certainly whatever you do,

NEVER SURPRISE

A BEAR."

The Human Being is capable of Superhuman Strength

Today school doesn't seem so bad—not as bad as before. I still do think Karl is acting weirdishly— he is still smiling at Clem Hansson in a hypnotized way and I catch him scowling at Justin Broach but at least we are talking again.

It's recess and I am walking across the playground. And I am walking past the bike sheds when I hear the whispering of Justin Broach. I can hear his lowish voice, saying, "I told you if you don't get me $20 then you won't get it back."

I stop very still.

The other voice is barely possible to hear and less low but I think it says, "But you said that last time and I did give you $20."

And the Justin Broach voice says, "Well, I'm

saying it *again,* aren't I?" And the other voice says, "But I don't have another $20, it was all I had."

And then Justin Broach says, "Well, why don't you give me that stupid hat?"

And then the quiet voice says, almost slightly sort of crying, "*No,* you can *never* have this hat—it was a *present.*"

And of course now I *know* I am right. It is Benji Murtle because he *does* have a funny hat. But I am surprised that he would not just hand over the hat if he wanted something else back so much. Benji Murtle normally does what people want him to do.

And the low voice says, "Well, it's up to you. Either you want Karneen back or you don't."

And then the second voice says, "How do I know you still have him?"

Instantly my ears are perked up because, you see, it is a very strange thing to say.

Who is Karneen?

Who has Justin Broach got?

And I can hear them coming around the side of the shed so I run for it because if Justin Broach knows I know something, then it will be me next

giving him my allowance—which by the way
I don't have.

When I get almost to the school door, I turn
around, and Benji Murtle is running back into class.
And then I see Justin Broach, and guess who is there
with him? *Clem Hansson,* and now I know I was
right about her—everyone thinks she is so nice, but
in fact she has been picking on Benji Murtle.

All afternoon I am wondering how I can make
Karl believe me—because, you see, he is not going
to like hearing that Clem Hansson is *not* super-nice
after all, and now I have proof.

I am so absorbed in wondering about this that
I get in big trouble with Mrs. Wilberton for not
paying attention and I have to stay behind cleaning
the board.

I go out the back way—past the bike sheds—
just in case I can catch up with Karl before he
cycles home.

There are a few people still around. Karl is one of
them, and so is Clem Hansson.
They aren't talking to each other, but Karl is sort of
hanging around.

Clem is just getting her bike—which is yellow.

It has stickers on it.

She is bending down to unlock it.

I decide to wait for her to go.

Justin Broach is hanging about too, and with him is the boy with the odd haircut—they are throwing acorns at each other and one *almost* hits Clem but she pretends she doesn't notice.

I see the boy with the odd haircut looking at Justin Broach in that way he looks.

Justin Broach throws another acorn, and this time it *does* hit Clem Hansson on the back and it is definitely on purpose.

I am surprised about this, because they are friends, and why is he throwing acorns at her?

She doesn't turn around or anything.

And I can tell this annoys him.

You see, he wants her to turn around because he wants to bother her, and if she isn't bothered, then the only thing he is good at isn't working.

He won't give up because he is like that—he is one of those people who never gives up.

And he is all jumpy.

And he keeps saying things, mean things.

And I don't understand what is going on.

And I think they must have had an argument.

But what have they been arguing about?

And the odd haircut boy just laughs.

And suddenly Justin Broach grabs Clem's hat and dangles it above a puddle like he is going to drop it in.

And Clem twirls around and she is red in the cheeks and her eyes have gone more pointy.

And she says, "*Give that back.*"

And I haven't seen her look like this—she is really mad and although her voice is not shouting, everyone looks around.

And the boy with the odd haircut looks at Justin Broach and for one second Justin Broach looks unsure.

And he goes to give it back and then suddenly he flings it up in the air and Clem's hat goes onto the bike-shed roof.

And Clem looks at him and she says, "My grandmother made that for me."

And she is upset and even so—she is not crying or anything—she just looks like she hates him.

And she is standing there looking at Justin Broach and he is trying to laugh, but he is rotten at laughing.

And then she gets on her bike and rides off.

And she doesn't turn around.

And I am *utterly* confused.

It's really bad and nobody else is laughing and Karl says, "You are such an idiot, Justin Broach." Then he says something much more ruder even and then he starts climbing up the shed and scrabbles onto the roof so just his legs are dangling a bit off the edge and he grabs hold of Clem's hat and just as he reaches it, Justin Broach pulls at Karl's leg and he is pulling and pulling and I start shouting, "Get off him, twit—you are going to pull him off."

But he won't stop and suddenly Karl just tumbles down and there is a bad sound.

He doesn't get up—he is just all crumpled on the ground.

Everybody is really quiet, and then slowly, Karl tries to stand up. He is a bit shaky and his face is palish as a sheet.

He is still clutching on to Clem's hat.

And he starts to get on his bike, but I can't help

noticing that there is something funny about his arm. Some of it is poking out in the wrong places.

And he is trying to ride off and I say, "Karl, I think that your arm is broken. I am going to get Mr. Skippard."

But Karl is not listening and I think he must be in shock. It's like Ruby Redfort says—**"The human being is capable of superhuman strength,"** and when you are almost dead or your arm is almost severed off, you can *still* ride a bike.

When I tell Mr. Skippard, he comes running out and luckily Karl has not gotten very far and Mr. Skippard is really calm—a bit like how my dad would be. My dad is an emergency person. You can't be with anybody better in an emergency, except maybe Uncle Ted.

And Mr. Skippard takes Karl off to the nurse's office and calls an ambulance. And everybody just stands around waiting until the ambulance comes and everybody watches the ambulance people put Karl in the back and Mr. Skippard goes with him because Karl's mom can't be contacted because she must be out dog-walking. And I feel sorry for Karl because even though Mr. Skippard is nice, I know Karl would like to have his mom with him.

I look down, and there is Clem's hat. Karl must have let go when the ambulance people lifted him in.

And I start to wonder about Clem Hansson and what is really going on with Justin Broach.

I pick it up—it is a bit muddy and I squash all the water out of it and then I walk back into school. I will hang it up on her peg, so it will be there tomorrow for when she gets in.

I wonder if I should really go over to her house and give it to her, because this way she would have it and not worry about it. But I don't feel like going over there—not now. I need to get home.

And as I am reaching up to her peg, I see something—it's just on the inside of the hat.

It's like a badge that you sew on.

And on the badge

there is

a fly.

Can you know Everything and Nothing at all?

By the time I get outside, it has started raining like mad, and I should have worn my slicker but who knew it was going to rain like this? Not the weatherman, anyway.

I can feel the wet soaking through my shoes, but I don't care.

I am thinking about Clem cycling off and how she looked when Justin Broach threw her hat onto the roof, and I remember how I overheard her talking to Karl and how it was a hat that her grandmother made her—and how her grandmother is now dead.

And I realize that Karl has remembered this too.

And I am beginning to realize I have made a big mistake.

The rain is trickling down between my collar and

my neck. It is icy cold and it feels like it could almost get through my skin—but luckily I am waterproof—we all are.

And I think, what is the point reading about all this survival information about lions and tigers and sharks? Why would I need to know how to find water in a desert? Or how to find dry land when I am lost at sea? *I live here on Navarino Street and these things are just not useful to know in my life.* Ruby Redfort just writes stupid adventure books; they are not for *real* people.

And I have read her **SPY GUIDE: HOW TO KNOW THINGS WITHOUT KNOWING THINGS**— and all I have discovered is that I know nothing at all. I thought I knew all about Clem Hansson, but I was wrong.

By the time I get home, the rain has got no more of me to soak into—so it is just dripping off onto the floor.

The only one home is Grandad—so I go up to my bedroom and search around for some dry socks, but no one has been doing any laundry lately so I

have to wear tights. I am rootling about in my sock
drawer trying to find ones without holes in them.
I pull out my favorite pair of stripy ones—the ones
that are the same as Betty Moody's—but when
I stick my leg in them, I can feel something flat
and papery.

I put my hand down inside and I pull out an
envelope and that's when I remember *Clem's
invitation*.

I haven't even looked at it.

When I open it, I see it is handmade by hand,
not by computer, and it has a red sort of heart design
on the front—I recognize this because it's a sort of
a Scandinavian thing that they do in Scandinavia.

Inside it says:

Please come to my party
on Saturday at 4 o'clock.
Wear whatever you like.
You don't have to bring a present~
it's up to you.
It would just be nice to see you.

Love from Clem

P.S. I really hope you can come.
I have only asked you and Karl.

It's all written in different colored felt-tips like a rainbow.

And on one side she has drawn the *Ruby Redfort fly* and on the other there is a tiny sticker of a rabbit—with an arrow pointing and the word **kanin**. It's a funny word and I wonder if it means *rabbit* in Swedish, or maybe it is just the name of *her* rabbit. And I am thinking about rabbits and rainbows and how Clem is always drawing rabbits and rainbows. And that reminds me of Karl, when I saw him in the shop and he was choosing a card of a rabbit and a rainbow for Clem for her birthday, and he bothered to go and I didn't, and that is why Karl was so mad at me. And that's why Clem didn't seem so keen to talk to me after fall break, because I hadn't bothered to go to her party—and I thought it was because she had become friends with Justin Broach and just wasn't interested in me.

But she never was friends with Justin Broach; all the time she was trying to be friends with me—and she sewed a Ruby fly badge into her hat, which she hoped I would notice because if I was a good Ruby spy, I would have seen and come to the rescue—

like Ruby does for Clancy Crew in
Run, Ruby, Run when she saves him from the
kidnappers . . . not that Clem has been *kidnapped*. . . .
And I pick up my Swedish dictionary—the one
that Uncle Ted's girlfriend gave me—and I look up
the word **kanin**.∗

    And it is in there and it tells you how you should
pronounce it kah-neen—it looks very different
from how it sounds,
and suddenly, I know something.
I know where I have heard that word before. I am
thinking about the voices behind the bike sheds. It
wasn't *Benji Murtle* who was in trouble with Justin
Broach. It wasn't *his* hat that he was trying to take.
It wasn't *Benji Murtle's* $20 that Justin Broach
wanted. It isn't something of *Benji Murtle's* that Justin
Broach has got. . . .

    It's something of Clem's.

    Justin Broach has got Clem's rabbit.

∗ **Kanin** [Kah-neen]—*is Swedish for rabbit*.

Don't Look now, but Look who it is

I am just staring and staring at the invitation. It's like Ruby Redfort so often says—all the pieces are coming together and making a different picture from the one I expected.

And I am wondering what I should do and then I remember something.

And I know who can help and I know who I must find.

And as I am thinking all this, I am pushing my bare feet into my boots and I am running down the stairs and I am grabbing my slicker and I am pushing my arms through the sleeves. I shout out to Grandad, "Where is Marcie? Is she out with Stan?"

And Grandad says, "She has gone to get me some eggs from the shop."

And I say, "But is she with Stan?"

And Grandad says, "I don't know, but she was with a girl with blue nails."

I say, "Stan?"

Grandad says, "Yes, Stan—they are getting me some eggs at the shop."

And I am out of the gate and I hear Grandad calling, "*Your laces are undone*,"

and I am running along the pavement to the end of the street,

and I am thinking all the time.

It's what Ruby's butler, Hitch, would always advise you to do in any survival emergency—"Just keep thinking, kid. The ones that keep thinking, they're the ones that survive."

And I am thinking how Karl tried to help Clem but it didn't work, so why do I think I can?

And I hear my feet stepping so fast along the pavement it's almost as if it's not me doing the running.

And I think of the man on the horse galloping along trying to distract the lion and of course I realize that is why Karl has been acting so strangely—

he has been trying to distract Justin Broach from bothering Clem and sometimes it works.

And sometimes it doesn't.

But at least he has been trying.

And I think of the man who stopped running from the tiger and just played dead—and by sort of ignoring it and not being afraid of it—it got bored and left him alone, because it was no fun anymore.

But ignoring Justin Broach has not worked for Clem. Nor has being friendly—like the way you might go up to a shark and swim actually toward it— like you aren't bothered.

But why hasn't distracting or ignoring or being friendly worked with Justin Broach, when it works with lions and tigers and sharks?

And I run faster and faster and my boots are rubbing the back of my ankles and I wish I had put my tights on. And I am getting nearer and nearer to Eggplant, and I don't want to miss Stan and Marcie and I decide to take the shortcut—up the little alley— although Mom says never go up the alley in the evening if you are on your own,
but this is an emergency.

And I can hear my feet making that echoey sound because it is such a narrow path and it's quite dark and I can just see two people standing at the top opposite Eggplant. One of them is shorter and one of them is taller. And I am relieved because it must be Marcie and Stan coming home and I have found them just in time.

And as I am running, I can feel my shoelace flipping.

And I keep thinking, lions tigers sharks.

And just as I think this thought I trip on my laces and go stumbling forward, and although I put my hands out to save me, I scrape my knee on the ground.

And I can feel right away that I have grazed my leg. I can't see it in the gloom but I know it will be oozing blood.

And then I hear a laugh.

It's the laugh of the boy with the odd haircut.

And when I look up, there is Justin Broach.

Never Surprise a Bear

33

Mom is right: never go up the little alley when it's dark. But it's too late now, and there I am trapped on the ground by Justin Broach.

And I can see the lights on in Eggplant and I can see Kira. She is kneeling in the shop window— sweeping up some flies probably.

And Justin Broach says, "Oh, look who it is, that *loser* Karl Wrenbury's friend."

I don't say anything.

He says, "So what have you got for me?"

And he sticks his hand in my coat pocket and pulls out a coin.

It's my emergency telephone money.

He says, *"Is this it?"*

And the boy with the odd haircut laughs.

And Justin Broach looks in my other pocket and pulls out the Polish cookie.

I had forgotten about that.

He says, "What kind of cookie do you call *this*?"

And he stuffs it in his mouth.

But I don't say anything.

I just stay still like Ruby Redfort says you should— "Stay still. Keep thinking. Don't panic."

And I am thinking about all the times I have avoided Justin Broach because I have had Betty Moody with me to say, "Don't look now, but look who it is."

But now I am all on my own.

And they are both looking at me in a mean way like the way they look at Benji Murtle and I think, *doing nothing* does not work with Justin Broach because he is not a tiger

  and distracting does not work
  because he is not a lion

    and being confident does not work
    because he is not a shark.

      But what is he?

And I don't know why I say it but it just comes out.

Because you see I've got to do something.

And I say,

"I know you have got Clem Hansson's rabbit."

And for the first time ever, Justin Broach looks really surprised—just for a tiny second.

And that's when I realize what Justin Broach is.

He is the most difficult thing of all.

Justin Broach is a bear.

And I know *you must never surprise a bear.*

But it's too late. He pulls me up by my coat.

And I feel the blood trickling down my leg from the cut on my knee.

And then he sees something,

it's my Ruby fly badge.

And he says, "That Hansson girl has got one of these. What's it for?"

And I don't say anything,

I am just trying to remember what you should do if you meet a bear.

And I wish Kira would look up.

If she did, she would see me,

she would *definitely* see me.

And Justin Broach says, "I think I will have this."

And he starts pulling the badge off my coat.

And I say, "No, you can't have my badge."

And he says,

"I   can   have   whatever   I   want."

And the only thing I can do is my Ruby hand signal—it is my only chance of getting Kira's attention.

It's a bit awkward to do in a natural kind of way.

And Kira isn't seeing.

And I wish she would look up.

And just as Justin Broach manages to grab my badge, a voice says, "What do you think you're doing, buster?" and a hand comes from nowhere and takes it off him.

It's Kira.

And Justin Broach says, "Oh, she was just giving me her badge."

Kira says, "Oh *right,* that sounds likely."

And she does her whistle, the one that Ruby Redfort can do—it's very loud. Suddenly Kurt pops his head out of the shop door and says, "What?" And then he sees me and comes over— he is still holding a tea towel in his hand from wiping down jars.

And Kira says, "These losers say your sister was giving them her badge."

And Kurt says, "My sister would never give them her Ruby badge."

Justin Broach looks scared and so does the other boy.

And I say, "They have got Clem Hansson's rabbit."

And Justin Broach says, "But I promise you I don't have it."

And then this voice says, "Yeah, you do."

It's Stan,

and when Justin Broach sees her, he looks really scared.

Stan says, "I've seen a rabbit in your backyard."

And Justin Broach says, "I am just looking after it."

And Stan says, "Justin, you might think everyone's stupid enough to believe your lies, but *I know you*— remember?"

And Justin Broach's eyes have gone all big, and he says, "It was just as a joke."

And Stan says, "Well, tell me, *who's laughing*?"

And Justin Broach doesn't answer.

Stan says, "I think your mom and dad are going to be in a pretty bad mood when they hear about this."

And Justin Broach goes white in the face and says, "Don't tell—please."

And Stan says, "Why wouldn't I?"

And Justin Broach is practically whimpering and he says, "I'll get it now—I promise. I'll take it back. Just don't tell my mom and dad."

And Stan says, "Well, Justin, that's up to *me,* isn't it?"

And she marches him off.

And he no longer looks like a bear— more like a weasel.

And I don't know where the boy with the odd haircut is, because he just seems to have disappeared.

And I remember what the woman on the radio said—*the more of you, the better*—when it comes to bears.

And suddenly I look around me and I am not on my own at all.

And I say to Kira, "Thanks for helping out."

And Kira says, "Anytime, kiddo."

And I say, "Why don't you come back with us once you have closed the shop . . . unless you are seeing Josh or something."

And Kira says, "Nah, we aren't together anymore."

And Kurt says, "Oh *great,* I mean, that's a shame—but *yeah,* come to our house."

And then he flicks her with his tea towel.

And she says,

"I'll get you for that, creep."

And they start doing their usual thing of messing around grabbing each other.

Just then, Marcie comes out of Foxes. She says, "Where's Stan gone? Hey, your leg is bleeding—how did that happen?" When I tell her she says, "Justin Broach? . . . Oh, Stan's cousin, he is *such* a weasel." Then she says, "Don't look now, but there goes that drip Amber."

And I say, "She's probably on her way to meet Kurt."

And Marcie says, "Nah, didn't you know? They're not together anymore."

When we get home, Dad says, "Guess what's cooking, kiddos?"

And I say, "Toast?"

And Grandad says, "Oh, that sounds nice."

And Dad says, "Well, too bad, you're getting chicken."

And Marcie says, "On toast?"

And Mom says, "Very funny—*look*! We've got a new oven."

Minal looks at Dad and says, "When are you getting divorced?"

And Dad says, "I wasn't aware that we were; no one told me about it."

And Mom says, "No, no one told *me* about it either."

And Minal says, "Clarice said you were."

And I say, "Little big-mouth."

And Dad says, "Clarice, are you *kidding*? I'm crazy about your mother."

And Mom says, "Thank you, darling. When you're not *driving* me crazy, I'm quite crazy about you."

And Marcie gives me this look, which I think means "*Get me outta here.*"

When you want to Run like Crazy, try Standing Still

34

Of course now that Karl is on painkillers with a broken arm, he will not be coming to the old persons' center with me.

I go over to his house, and Alf answers the door.

I say, "How is Karl?"

And Alf says, "He is taking pills."

When I go in, Karl looks palish and he sounds a bit shaky.

He says, "Watcha, CB. What's been going on?"

I say, "This and that—quite a lot, actually."

And then I tell him about Justin and the rabbit and how Stan marched him over to Clem's house and made him give it back and say sorry, which Justin Broach doesn't normally do.

And Karl says, "*Wow,* CB, how did you find out?"

And I say, "Well, I have been reading **THE RUBY REDFORT SPY GUIDE: HOW TO KNOW THINGS WITHOUT KNOWING THINGS**. It's full of useful and important information."

Karl says, "But why didn't Clem tell somebody?"

And Alf says, "Yes, she should have told somebody."

And I say, "But Justin Broach probably said that if she told, she would never see her rabbit again. This kind of thing happens in Ruby Redfort all the time."

And Karl says, "You're right, because Clem must have been really scared of Justin Broach."

And I say, "But I thought he was being all friendly to her and she liked him."

And Karl says, "But you know what Justin Broach is like; that's what he wants you to think—he is sneaky."

And Alf says, "Yes, he is sneaky."

And Karl says, "He kept on doing things like stealing her gym clothes and eating her lunch and throwing her bag on the ground, but he always does it mainly when no one is looking."

And now that Karl is telling me, I can see everything—and of course, Justin Broach put that green marker in Clem's pocket so she would get into trouble.

And I fell for it. And I say, "I don't think I would make a very good spy."

And Karl says, "Well, you got her rabbit back, didn't you? She must be really happy you did that."

And I say, "Well, I didn't tell her it was me who discovered it—I feel too bad because she must think I am a dreadfulish person who is not nice enough to even open her invitation."

And he says, "Yeah, but you got her *rabbit* back."

And Alf says, "You got her rabbit back."

Then Karl says, "I am really sorry I can't come to visit Mr. Larsson with you."

And I say, "Don't worry—I am sure he isn't that bad."

And Karl says, "No, I expect he is really nice."

And I say, "Deep down, you mean."

And Alf says, "Quite a lot deep down."

And Kurt says, "Yes, once you really get to know him."

And I say, "Yes, once I get to know him, I am sure we will be great friends."

And Alf looks sideways at Karl.

And Karl says, "So long as you don't offer him dessert."

And I say, "Yes, no desserts—especially trifle."

And he says, "And if you do offer him a dessert, don't forget to duck."

And Alf says, "Yes, don't forget to duck."

On the day of the visit, it all doesn't seem quite so funny, and I think of Karl watching TV with Alf, and I wish I was them.

Mom has dropped me off in front by the doors, she is parking the car and I am trying to balance a whole tray of cookies, raisiny ones, on one arm and also hold my bag and present for Mr. Larsson with the other. I have gotten him a Ruby pen which also tells you the temperature of the weather. Mom says he could use this because he is always going outside without enough warm clothes—he says the weather in this country is nothing compared to what he is used to—we just don't know what cold is over here. I wish Mom would hurry up because my tights are doing that thing where they sort of slip down a bit so you get the feeling that your legs are joined together at the actual knees. Also it is cold—very cold—even if Mr. Larsson wouldn't think so. Mom finally arrives and we walk into the building— neither of us is talking because Mom is too busy trying to make sure she has remembered everything, and I am too busy worrying how Mr. Larsson might fling a dessert at me and then I think about Karl's mom's turtle—and where did it go and did Mr. Larsson actually eat it? And then I am really sweating.

I make my pot of tea and put my cookies on a plate—in the pattern of a star, because I hope he might think this looks Christmassy and decide to have more goodwill for all mankind. Mom has brought our dog Cement in to see Mr. Enkledorf and he is trying to lick the cookies. I have saved a couple of them for Mr. Flanders because, as a cookie expert, he would be interested in their strange shape.

I am walking really slowly down the corridor with the clattery tray and the teapot is slightly spilling out at the spout and getting into the sugar—so it is a bit wet, and I think, I bet Mr. Larsson won't like that. And I am hoping it hasn't gone onto the cookies because I made them myself and although they are not very round, they do taste good and I have put ginger in them because I know Mr. Larsson likes things to taste of ginger.

And all the time I am thinking I wish I wasn't here—and I pass Mr. Flanders' door and he is playing nice music, piano-ish music. Then I pass Mrs. Lovett's door and Mr. Enkledorf's and I keep going right to the end of the corridor. And I am standing there with the tray balanced and I am thinking about not knocking—just putting the tray down and running. Like Ruby would say when you meet an unfriendly life-form, "Run like crazy."

But I don't.

I take a very deep breath and I knock— three knocks.

And I think if he doesn't answer by the time I have counted to ten—then I will go. And I count

1 2 3 4 5 6 7 8 9 . . .

And just before **10**, I hear some shuffling and an old voice says, "*Come in.*"

And my hand is on the handle and I am about to turn it when I feel a tiny tap on my arm—I don't even realize it is a tap at first,

until someone says,

"Clarice Bean,
I wondered if I could
be in a pair with you."

And I turn around and it is Clem Hansson.

And before I can say anything, Mr. Larsson creaks open the door and says,

"Come in if you're coming."

Someone will Always notice the Unnoticable— in the End

I stand there looking up at Mr. Larsson. He is a very tall man—even when he is all stooped over. And he does not have a very friendly face—more of a scowl. But what I do is something Ruby Redfort would advise—I "grin until it hurts." And I say, "Hello, Mr. Larsson. I am Clarice Bean and this is Clem."

And then Clem says, "**Hejsan**, Mr. Larsson."

And I know from Uncle Ted's girlfriend, Stina, that this means hello in Swedish.

And Mr. Larsson looks quite surprised for almost 2 seconds and says, "**Hejsan**" back.

And then Clem and Mr. Larsson talk to each other in Swedish and I know some words but not others, so I don't know exactly what they are saying, but

I can tell from the way that they are saying it that Mr. Larsson is not going to fling any desserts.

Then Mr. Larsson looks at the tray and says to me, "What lovely looking cookies, are they ginger?"

And I say, "Yes, they are in fact, or at least slightly—because they didn't start off ginger until I remembered that you liked ginger so I added it in at the end."

And Mr. Larsson says, "How thoughtful, how did you know I liked ginger?"

And I realize I don't want to tell him about how I know he flung his dessert because a dog ate his gingerbread, so I say, "I just heard."

We have our cups of tea—although mine is just a cup of milk, because I do not drink tea actually and I have decided to stop pretending I do, and we chat for a bit in English and Swedish.

I say, "**Det är en spindel i mitt rum**,"✳ because it is the only phrase I know.

Mr. Larsson says, "I also have a spider in my room, and I wish it would go away because I do not like spiders."

Clem says, "Neither do I."

✳ *"There is a spider in my room."*

I say, "I will get him out for you if you like. I am not too worried by spiders." I pick it up with my *bare hands* and having two people more afraid of spiders than I am stops me from being afraid.

I can tell he is very impressed and so is Clem.

And then Clem asks him how come he moved here in the first place, and he says it's because his daughter wanted him to live over here with her because she was worried about him being all on his own in Sweden.

And Clem says she is here because her dad has a job to do with the environment and he is going to work on our environment over here.

And they talk about Sweden and Mr. Larsson says he misses it dreadfully.

And I am beginning to understand why he has been being unfriendly, because when you are sad you don't feel so nice—you sort of want everyone to leave you alone even though at the same time you wish people would talk to you.

And I think how it must be very hard for Clem to come to this country and be nice when all the time she wishes she wasn't here. And then I think about

Betty and how she must feel all the way off on her own in San Francisco, and I decide that I will e-mail her as soon as I get home.

Just before we go I say, "I got you this present." And I give him my Ruby Redfort pen with the temperature thingy and he says he has never been given anything so useful.

Mr. Larsson says he has very much enjoyed our visit and he hopes we will come and see him again.

And I say, maybe he can come to our house one time—it's nice to get out.

And he says, "**Tak**," which means thank you.

And I say, "**Varsågod**"—which means you're welcome.

When we are outside, I say to Clem, "How did you know that Mr. Larsson was Swedish?" And she says, "His *name* is Swedish."

And I say, "I am sorry I missed your party and I am sorry I thought you were a friend of Justin Broach."

And she says, "That's OK."

And I say, "If I'd noticed your fly badge, I would have known you could not be friends with him."

And she says, "I know."

And I say, "Have you got the new Ruby books? I have the **SPY GUIDE** and the **SURVIVAL HANDBOOK**—you can borrow them if you want."

She says, "I'd like that."

And I say, "Well, thanks for coming to see Mr. Larsson with me—I was a bit nervous."

She says, "**Varsågod**."

And then we say good-bye and I realize she is not someone who is a chatterbox, and I quite like that—she is more like Hitch than Ruby.

And I have walked halfway down the sidewalk and she calls out, "Thanks for rescuing my rabbit," and I shout, "But how did you know it was me?" and she says, "Stan told me—anyway I saw your Ruby badge and I knew that in the end you would come to the rescue."

When I get home, I shout out, "**Cześć**."*

And Jacek shouts, "**Tutaj**."*

Hello and *Up here in Polish.*

245

He is busy painting my room—it's bright white
and so is the floor and although it is just meant to
be the undercoat, I think it really looks very nice.
Sort of spacious, even though it is a very small sort
of spacious.

I tell Jacek about the wobbly floorboard and
how it has gone and now I can't get my book.
What he does is take out the nails and lift up
the board and there they are,
my book and my **Run, Ruby, Run** tickets.

He says he can leave it wobbly if I like.

And I say, "OK."

When he has gone I look at the tickets—
the date is coming up very soon—it's next week.

I go downstairs and I phone Clem and I say,
"Are you busy next Friday?" And she says,
"No, why?" And I say,
"Oh, just thought you might want to meet up,
that's all." And she says,
"Yes, I would. What would you like to do?"

And I say, "Nothing special."

Maybe infinity is not such a big worry after all

I talked to Betty on the telephone last week.

It was nice to hear her voice again, and she sounded really happy to hear mine.

I told her what had been going on and she said she was sorry to miss it—it all sounded very exciting.

I said it was a bit like the Macey Gruber story I had been writing and that it has given me an idea for how I might do the end.

And it was no wonder that it was so hard to come up with a twist, because I never would have thought that this could possibly have happened in a story, let alone real life.

And Betty agreed and said it's funny that sometimes real life is more extraordinary than a Macey Gruber

story or even an actual Ruby Redfort book,
and I guess that is the good thing about life—there is
always more than one twist.

I asked her if she had been to see the bears yet and
she said no, not yet.

And I told her to read Ruby's **SURVIVAL
HANDBOOK** before she goes because bears can be
tricky and she said yes, she would.

We talked some more about Clem—and Betty's
new friend Quincy, and how we would all most
probably like each other.

And she said it's funny how you can not like
someone so much and then when you get to know
them, you really do.

And I agreed that life can be very surprising.

She said she was really sorry to be missing the
Run, Ruby, Run premiere and that she was really
impressed that I had managed to keep it a secret
surprise for Clem. And would I please be sure to take
some photos of me and Skyler Summer—
and I said, "You can count on it, kid."

And it was sad to say good-bye but we had talked
for an hour and seventeen minutes nonstop and Mom

said it would be cheaper to send me there at this rate, so maybe they will—who knows?

I have started saving up.

When I put down the phone, I went right up to the attic. And I sat on Betty's beanbag just looking at my room for a few minutes, maybe sevenish, and I was pleased with how all my things looked in there.

I have decided to keep it mainly white—I find it very good for sleeping, and Mom has said I can draw on the walls if I want to because it is completely my space. So far I have drawn a fly and next to it is a photograph of me and Betty.

Then I opened the window and looked up at the stars—it was a very chilly night and so it was clearer than usual, so the sky looked higher up.

And I thought about this astronaut I heard talking on my radio about what it is like up in space.

And he said it made him feel very calm, because you just looked out of the window of your rocket and all you saw for miles and miles was just stars and it was a comfort somehow to realize that the universe was such a big place and that the human-being race are just mere insects on a tiny sphere spinning away in the galaxy.

It seemed like all the stars were out and I thought to myself, all these stars can also be seen by Betty Moody — not now because it is day for her but when it is her nighttime, she will be able to see a lot of the same stars I can.

And I realized that although the world can feel like a very big place and people can seem very far away, it is also true that the world is a very small place.

And maybe that is the point of infinity — that it is there to remind you that things on this world aren't as big as you think they are — not compared to infinity, anyway. Because, you see, Betty Moody compared to infinity is practically next door.

And I am beginning to think maybe infinity is not such a big worry after all.

I pick up **THE RUBY REDFORT SURVIVAL HANDBOOK** *because I am interested to see what she says about bears and I have to flick right through the book, and as I am flicking through, I find a page right at the end that seems to be stuck together and when I look at it more closely, I notice that it says in tiny, tiny type so you can hardly see it . . .*

SO YOU WANNA KNOW WHAT TO DO ABOUT THE WORST WORRY YOU NEVER EVEN THOUGHT TO WORRY ABOUT?

tear here ↗

And when I do,
when I tear it open—
this is what it says,

The trick is—
don't lose sleep
over it, kid.

Gina *Lauren*

For Gina, my first ever best friend.

Thank you to Ann-Janine Murtagh, Alice Blacker,
David Mackintosh, Trisha and Rachel.
And to anyone who might have broken an arm
falling off a bike-shed roof—
especially Adrian.

Hey, buster, why don't you visit:
www.candlewick.com